The Rich Die Young

The Rich Die Young

Carolyn G. Hart

Five Star
Unity, Maine

Five Star First Edition Mystery Series

First Edition, Second Printing

Published in 2000 in conjunction with Tekno Books and Ed Gorman.

The text of this edition is unabridged.

Set in 11 pt. Plantin by Anne Bradeen.

Printed in the United States on permanent paper.

Library of Congress Cataloging-in-Publication Data

Hart, Carolyn G.
    The rich die young / by Carolyn G. Hart.
        p.   cm.
    ISBN 0-7862-2898-9 (hc : alk. paper)
    1. Women college teachers —Fiction. 2. California,
Southern—Fiction. 3. Police—California, Southern
—Fiction. I. Title.
PS3558.A676 R53 2000
813'.54—dc21   00-061030

The Rich Die Young

ONE

What in the world was I doing here? I stopped halfway across the humped wooden bridge that spanned Lovers' Pond. Students swept by, laughing, talking, good-naturedly pushing and teasing, and I felt completely out of place.

It wasn't that my surroundings were foreign. No, they were so familiar. This was home. Sunny Southern California. Though not so sunny in January. The water was grey and the sky and my thoughts. Grey sky, grey world, grey . . .

Oh, come on, Ann!

I smiled despite my gloom. I'm not cut out for heavy drama. I'm too quick to see the absurd. Especially when I am the protagonist.

That was a ten-dollar word. That's what Michael would have scrawled on my copy. I took a deep breath and turned and crossed on over the bridge. I would not think of Michael.

I looked up then, looked across the familiar rugged landscape, at the paths twisting up and down, at the cream-coloured adobe buildings built so cunningly into the hillside. Even on a bleached-out winter day, Friars' Academy was beautiful.

But it wasn't at all as I remembered it.

"Ms. Farrell! Ms. Farrell!"

I stopped and looked back. Katie Bernstein came rushing down the crumbling steps from the terrace that overlooked the ravine.

She skidded to a stop beside me, "Ms. Farrell, Oscar's hunting for you."

"Oh."

She understood that uninflected 'oh' immediately.

"It's all right," she said quickly. "He isn't stoned. He seemed . . ." She paused, her fine black eyebrows drawing together, "he seemed anxious."

Oscar. An anxious Oscar. He had sat in my morning editing class this past year, staring off into space, his handsome heavy face utterly blank, like a piece of plexiglass. I looked inquiringly at Katie.

"Anxious," she repeated. "Excited."

Excitement was another emotion foreign to the Oscar I knew. Though I had, several times recently, actually communicated with him when he wasn't wrapped in a haze of pot.

"He really wants you to come." The first bell rang and Katie dashed ahead.

Michael would have liked Katie.

The paths were empty now, everyone corralled in class. I walked alone, slowly, and one more time heard in my mind the rattle of rifle fire. I had told Michael not to go out that day. Somehow I'd known. But he'd grabbed his notebook and shrugged away my warning.

The helicopter took off from San Salvador on a bright sunny morning. It never came back. They found its charred hulk five days later. I'd left five days later, coming home to California, white, stricken, hopeless. I'd taken long walks alone and never mentioned Michael's name. Then Mother told me Friars' Academy was looking for an unmarried teacher to live on the campus in one of the residence halls. Most students at Friars' Academy were day students but there were two halls for boarders.

It was a place to live while I patched my life back together.

I came to the fork in the path and hesitated. If I turned right, I would reach a rock stairway leading down to the two-storey circular building that housed the *Herald* and, also, my office and classroom.

I did love that building. It was built into the hillside and had huge curving windows that overlooked the ravine. Inside, the bottom storey contained the news-room with a horseshoe for copy-editors and rows of ramshackle desks with type-writers for the reporters. Friars' Academy had the latest in equipment for the art and science departments but it didn't run to electronic machines for the journalism department. But my kids had lots of years yet to learn how to write on machines.

My office was upstairs, a huge room half filled with filing cabinets. But the other half was open and spacious with only my desk and chair. It was a little like officing in a cloud. On misty days, when fog wreathed the hillside, droplets of mist condensed against the windows and I seemed to hang in the sky like an eagle. On clear days, the sunlight glistened on the hillside that fell away so sharply beneath me.

I needed to go back to the office to lock it up for the night. But I didn't want to talk to Oscar. I glanced at my watch. Just after three.

The rain decided me. It began to sweep across the barranca toward the hillside, a fine grey curtain. I turned to my left and dashed for the staircase that led up to the terrace. Most of the year, the terrace is the heart of the campus but the January rains had left scattered pools of water and the brightly coloured polyethylene chairs and settees were lined disconsolately against one adobe wall, waiting for sunshine.

I burst into the dining-room just as the rain began to slap against the tile paving of the terrace. The dining-room was closed, of course, but the snack-bar with self-serve coffee urns and trays of Danishes stayed open until five. I drew a mug of coffee and, after judicious study, selected a caramel long john and dropped fifty cents in the shallow ceramic tray next to the hooded cash register.

"Hey, Ann!"

I looked up. Dodie Wingate waved.

Then I was settled across from her, my purse and raincoat hung over an empty chair. I saw her staring mournfully at my plate.

"It isn't enough," she said dourly, "to endure the January rains, the post-Christmas depressions, the generally asocial decline of personalities before midwinter break, no, I must become friends with a slim young thing who flaunts her youth by eating caramel long johns in front of her portly elders."

I grinned. Dodie is a frank forty-five with blowsy red hair, an ample figure and a commonsense nature. She is tremendously successful as a counsellor, partly because she is always low key and absolutely unshockable.

I took a huge bite and mumbled, "Think how superior you will feel when you resist temptation . . ." but she was already pushing back her chair. When she rejoined me with a chocolate long john, she said quickly, "Eat now, repent later."

When she was finished, she leaned back in her chair and sighed. "I should now begin to feel better. Sugar pulsing into my bloodstream." She sighed again. "Except it's only temporary."

"Everything's temporary."

She cocked her head at me. "Out of the mouths of babes. But that's profound, Ann. Damn, I'm glad you came and sat down here."

"Always good for one cheer-up a day."

"I wish you would spread it around."

"Work getting you down?"

Her thick reddish eyebrows drew together. "Yes, I guess that's it. Except it's more than that. And it's more than the post-Christmas blahs. Or even the lousy weather. All of that happens every January and I have at least one threatened suicide, a couple of drug o.d.s, occasionally some v.d. Of course, this year there was that awful thing about Bitsy Martin. But there's something more. Something wrong."

I looked at her curiously. "What do you mean?"

She ran a pudgy hand through her thick red hair. "I'll be dammed if I know what I mean, Ann. But I've worked here, my God, it's ten years now. I remember you as a sophomore my first year. And there's something wrong!"

I drank another sip of coffee. I knew what Ann was talking about. A malaise permeated the campus.

"Like that faculty meeting yesterday," Dodie exclaimed.

I nodded. That had indeed been a peculiar meeting. To begin, there was none of the usual amiable bickering as everyone sank into place. It was quiet. Sullenly, tensely quiet. I'd wondered for a moment, as I sat down, whether there was going to be a firing or an execution. But Dr. Howard began in his customary pleasant manner. He smiled genially. No one smiled back.

For a moment, Dr. Howard looked nonplussed, then, smoothly, he slipped into a brisk discussion of finances.

I disengaged my mind and began a pleasant fantasy involving Steve Tibbets, the new track coach, who stood six three in his socks. Abruptly, I was shocked back to attention.

Belinda Bascomb, the ceramics teacher, pushed back her chair and jumped to her feet. Belinda ordinarily was pretty if you don't mind a vacuous face and a little girl voice. Now her round face with its frame of ringleted yellow hair was suffused an ugly pinkish-red.

Dr. Howard looked absolutely stunned. As did everyone else.

"I asked . . . that is, please, Miss Bascomb, you must have misunderstood me. I was inquiring about the usage of the art lounge in the evenings."

Belinda looked at Dr. Howard, tears streaming down her face. "No one understands . . ."

Then she ran out of the library.

It was utterly quiet.

Clay came to the rescue. "Gene, if I may say a word."

"Oh yes, Clay, of course," Dr. Howard said gratefully.

"I wondered if we might have some input on next fall's holiday schedule." Clay suggested a date alteration, then smiled. It was the same magical smile that had enthralled at least a decade of Friars' Academy girls.

It always made everyone feel better.

"I wonder what would have happened if Clay hadn't spoken up?" I asked Dodie.

"I wonder, too." She frowned. "Damn him, if he'd kept quiet, I think it might all have broken loose."

"What would have broken loose?"

Dodie spread her hands helplessly. "I don't know exactly, Ann. It's just that I think whatever it is that's bugging everybody might have come out in the open. Clay must have sensed that too. And that's interesting, isn't it?"

"Clay's pretty perceptive . . ."

She was shaking her head. "No, that isn't what I mean. Sure, he's perceptive. Clay always knows which way to jump. . . ."

I realized with a sense of shock that Dodie didn't like Clay. Urbane, charming handsome Clay.

". . . no, what interests me is that he was so determined to keep the lid on. I wonder why?"

12

Clay was the kind of man who abhorred scenes. "He just didn't want to dwell on Belinda's breakdown."

Dodie shrugged. "Maybe." She looked past me at the windows overlooking the terrace, the panes opaque with rain, and sighed. "If this damn rain doesn't stop, my house is going to slide into a canyon."

"California may slide into a canyon."

She almost managed a smile. Slides aren't too mirth-provoking out here.

When she was gone, I stirred the dregs of my coffee. The door from the terrace opened and a wash of rain and Paul Casteel came in. Now if it had been the new track coach . . . I took a final sip of coffee and pushed back my chair. I was in no mood for a tête-à-tête with Paul Casteel.

But Paul apparently hadn't seen me.

Surely he had. I was wearing vivid red slacks and I was the only person drinking coffee in the whole long room.

Any second he would swing around and call out in his high soft voice, "Sweetie, how beautiful you are today!" and clap his hands together in exaggerated surprise.

It wasn't that Paul was so queer, though he assuredly was, that scattered everyone in his vicinity, it was his non-stop, mechanical chatter, that, with the exception of a few phrases of greeting or dismissal, consisted solely of self-adulation. Paul, in short, was a monumental bore.

He strode, head down, toward the door by the snack-bar. His long thin, fair hair, usually curled and combed in a pompadour, was plastered against his narrow head. He really was drenched. Maybe that accounted for his uncharacteristic behaviour. And for the thin tight mouth and pale set face. Then, so quickly I almost missed it, he looked around the room. He saw me, I was sure of it, but he averted his eyes and walked a little faster toward the exit.

I slipped into my raincoat. Paul's peculiar performance capped a strange day, and, again, I realized that coming back to Friars' Academy was a mistake. It wasn't the place I remembered. I paused for a moment at the door to the terrace and looked out of the rain-spangled windows. At the beginning of the fall semester, it had seemed like the Academy I knew. The faculty seemed familiar, too. But not for long. I wasn't a student now and there was a difference in manner and, finally, a difference in perception. I had always thought Dr. Howard, despite his pleasant manner, almost an august personage. He was, actually, just a middle-aged school administrator troubled by inflation and haemorrhoids. And Jennifer Prince. When I was in school, she was Miss Prince and I studied hard in her English classes. She had beautiful diction and could hold the attention of any class as she read in her deep bell-clear voice. Now she was Jennifer and I learned that she liked to make the singles bars and kept a bottle of vodka in the teachers' lounge.

Just because all is not green and glorious in Eden doesn't mean it's all slimy, either. It was a jolt to realize they were ordinary people and some of them not very attractive ones.

So I needed to be looking around for a job. One where my past didn't keep stumbling over my present and I didn't feel an ache every time another illusion crumbled. Besides, fun though it was to teach, it wasn't my thing. I was a reporter. I would go back to it. Michael would expect it of me.

The rain was beginning to slack now. A rainbow curved suddenly over the barranca. I pushed out onto the terrace. I didn't pass anyone as I walked to the *Herald* office. Surely Oscar had given up by now. Several times recently, Oscar had stayed at his typewriter after the other students had left.

I sat in the curve of the horseshoe, editing copy for next week's *Herald*.

14

"Ms. Farrell?"

"Yes, Oscar."

"Somebody told me you were a reporter."

"Yes."

"I mean, a real one. With a wire service in San Salvador during the fighting and everything."

"That's right."

"Was it exciting?"

Oh, Michael.

"It was . . . I didn't like it, Oscar. Someone I liked very much was killed."

"Oh, Ms. Farrell. Gee, I'm sorry. I didn't mean to say the wrong thing."

I looked at him through a hot sting of tears. How long would it be before I didn't cry?

"Oh, Ms. Farrell, I'm real sorry."

"That's all right, Oscar."

That was the beginning of our occasional odd conferences. Usually, of course, he sat in class, his mind fogged, reeking of marijuana. But once or twice he had stayed late and been alert and I had hoped for him. You always hope for the ones really into pot. You hope they will outgrow it, leave the heavy daily smoking behind. It's like everything else, there are plenty who never touch it, lots who smoke it now and again and remain unscathed, and, always, the Oscars.

These last few weeks, though, there was a real change in Oscar and it puzzled me. He wasn't smoking pot, but still he sat in class, his face heavy, staring out at something no one else could see with a sullen anger in his eyes.

The late afternoon sun, shining palely through slitted pink clouds, glistened on the curving windows of my building, I couldn't tell whether there was a light on inside. Was Oscar still there? Surely he had given up.

15

I pulled down on the iron bar that served as a knob on the heavy wooden door. The door creaked slowly in. It was a little like coming into a lighthouse, the stairs to the second floor curving up the left, a narrow passageway curving to the right, leading into the news-room.

I checked automatically, as I rounded the corner and passed the rows of typewriters, making sure no one had left on an electric typewriter. And, yes, there toward the back, Oscar's typewriter faintly hummed. A sheet of yellow copy was still in the carriage. I leaned over, flicked the typewriter off, and noticed without any particular interest that he had typed haphazardly on the sheet with no coherence or pattern, like pencilled doodlings on scrap paper.

I gave the room another swift survey, then I turned off the lights and went back around to the front to go up the stairs to the second floor and my office.

The late afternoon sun flooded through the curving bank of windows, touching my desk with gold, and making quite prominent the once-folded sheet of pink paper that broke its clear expanse.

Like all institutions, Friars' Academy has its little ways. Blue slips for commendation. White slips for inter-office memos. Pink slips for warning.

It didn't signal anything to me, that loosely folded pink slip, lying on my desktop.

I saw my name, Ms. Farrell, scrawled in black letters across the back. I picked it up, unfolded the slip, saw the printed heading, OFFICIAL WARNING, and saw, too, the handwritten message in thick uneven block letters:

WOULDN'T CLAY FREDERICKS' WIFE LIKE TO KNOW ABOUT YOU? CALAVETTI MOTEL, NOVEMBER 23.

HUSSY! ! ! !

16

TWO

Oh, good grief!

A rush of furious embarrassment swept me. My face flamed.

Could people possibly believe . . . Faces flashed through my mind—Dr. Howard when he nodded at me before the faculty meeting started, Dodie Wingate at coffee, Alice Calhoun when she dropped by the minutes of the Chemistry Club meeting. All of them had treated me just as usual. And June Fredericks, Clay's wife. She had waved casually last week-end as I crossed their tennis court after finishing a set. June's greeting had been cool, but June was always cool. Understated, unruffled, her blond hair swept up into a thick coil that stayed sleek and perfect even after three sets of tennis, she never looked hot or tired or bedraggled. Perfect, perfect June.

I would feel like such an utter fool if June Fredericks knew.

The sun slipped behind the hilltop and it was abruptly dim in my office and chilly. I shivered. Obviously, someone had seen Clay and me at the motel. Just as obviously, they didn't know the evening's outcome.

Did the writer intend to frighten me? Was a copy going to June Fredericks?

Well, chickens do have a way of coming home to roost. This could all be very awkward and unpleasant and acutely embarrassing, but keeping my job here wasn't a life or death matter.

17

HUSSY. What a fine, old-fashioned, mouthfilling term of vituperation. Damn near Dickensian. Hussy was not a word I would expect my compatriots to use. Of course, until tonight, I wouldn't have expected to find the author of an anonymous letter among my acquaintances.

Someone I knew . . .

I crumpled the slip into a rough-edged ball.

Downstairs, the entrance door creaked open.

I waited by my desk.

But the footsteps below went into the newsroom, not up my stairs. I didn't call out. I didn't want to see anyone. Not now.

I held my breath when the footsteps sounded again, but the walker didn't turn up the stairs and, in a moment, I heard the front door creak shut.

I waited for fine minutes, then hurried downstairs. I locked the door and turned toward the dark path to McDonough Hall. The campus lay absolutely quiet now, even the last of the varsity athletes gone. An occasional light in a classroom marked the progress of the night-cleaning crew.

McDonough Hall had not, of course, belonged with the original monastery buildings. It was a good five minute walk from the campus, part of it over a swaying footbridge with rope handrails that crossed the ravine. A hundred yards to the right was a wooden bridge for cars. The front porch light was on, illuminating the hall's scrolled gables and bracketed verandah and bright orange paint. My suite, a room, bath and kitchenette, was actually in a turret. I was climbing the broad shallow steps to the verandah when I stopped, looked at the leaded windows on either side of the front door, then turned and started back down.

I didn't want to see anyone connected with the school. But

18

I certainly didn't want to be alone.

I almost ran toward the narrow parking lot bordered by eucalyptus trees. I drove out of the lot and across the wooden bridge onto the campus and followed the back loop to the main drive. I drove fast to the canyon road and plunged down the narrow, twisty blacktop. I sped on into LA and, on impulse, dropped by the Carey School of Dance. Sheila was just finishing with a class of six-year-olds. She slipped on levis and we went out to dinner, then drifted on into the bar and drank spritzers.

I drove back up into the hills in a fairly mellow glow. The note was something that had happened but right this minute it didn't seem all that overwhelming. Anyway, I would think about it tomorrow.

Coming back onto the campus, the main drive passed the student parking-area which spread off to the right. Since the boulevard was divided, with a hedge of oleanders down the centre, I hadn't been able to see the lot earlier. Now, driving fairly slowly, not thinking of anything but a good dinner and Sheila's diverting chatter, I glanced casually to my right and saw a car at the far end of the lot. Funny. Somebody must have had battery . . . I began to brake.

Not battery trouble. Not with that car. I backed the Rabbit up then turned off into the lot and drove so fast the tyres screeched when I slammed to a stop beside the midnight blue Maserati. I jumped out and ran to the driver's side and peered inside. It was empty.

Why had Oscar left his car?

I knew the answer to that one. Oscar hadn't left his car. If the Maserati was in the lot, Oscar was somewhere on the campus. I didn't think there was much love in Oscar's life. Like many of the very, very rich, there was little he didn't have or hadn't done so he was very casual about two hundred

19

dollar cashmere sweaters and week-end flights to Mexico City. He was not casual about his Maserati. She glistened with turtle wax. Her leather shone from soft repeated strokes. He loved to talk about how she handled, how she could hug a curve at ninety-five. If there was one thing that Oscar valued, it was his incomparable Maserati.

I stood uncertainly by the sleek lovely car, my hand lightly touching the door panel, so cold and moist from the foggy night air. Then I looked across the lot toward the barranca.

The Maserati was not in the most convenient spot for access to the general campus. But, on a direct line, it was the very closest place a student could park to walk to the *Herald* office. I could see, through a line of cedars, the curving adobe walls and the dark glisten of the windows.

"Oscar . . ."

He had been looking for me. Oh Lord, what if . . . I didn't want to put it into words. Frantically, I turned and ran toward the Rabbit and got the flashlight out of the dash compartment.

The beam of the flashlight dipped and swayed as I ran toward the round building. Katie said Oscar wasn't stoned. But what if he kept looking for me, needing someone to talk to, and, when there was no one, when he was alone and the rain swept greyly across the ravine, what if he had overdosed? That happened in January, that's what Dodie had said, always one or two o.d.s in January . . . Oh God, please, I was going to talk to Oscar tomorrow. Don't make it too late. Please God, he's only seventeen and I was going to talk to him tomorrow . . .

I was breathless, my heart thudding, by the time I reached the office. I jammed the huge key into the lock, pulled down the bar and pushed in the door. I plunged into the hallway and ran down the curved passageway into the news-room.

When the lights were on, I looked in every corner, checked every cupboard and the dark shadow behind the horseshoe. Still breathing fast, I stopped by the rack holding *The New York Times.*

All right, he's not here. Oscar's not here. But he wouldn't leave his Maserati. He's here somewhere. On the campus.

I felt a wave of nausea. Should I call the night-watchman, insist he help me search? Search what? The entire damn twenty-acre campus? No, he wouldn't do it.

Call. That's it. I'd call Oscar's house. Maybe there was an explanation. Maybe the Maserati, the perfect car, had failed for once.

Oscar wouldn't have left her. Hell, he would hire a service station, the Maserati franchise, the world, before he would leave that car.

I grabbed up a student directory.

HOWELL, OSCAR CHARLES II. 93 Arrowhead Road. 835-0742.

I reached for the telephone, then hesitated. It was a quarter past midnight. But these kids stayed up forever.

I dialled. A thick sleepy voice answered at the eighth ring.

"Oscar? One moment, please. I will ring his room."

So the butler had answered. Imagine living in an establishment that had even a modest switchboard.

I heard the buzzes. At the ninth or tenth buzz, I gave up hope. Oscar wasn't there.

"There is no answer in Mr. Oscar's room." The voice wasn't sleepy now, merely resigned.

"Please, will you see if he is there."

"Miss, he didn't answer."

"But he should be there, shouldn't he?"

There was a pause. "I will see, Miss."

I waited. I waited five minutes, seven, and I wondered how

21

large Oscar's home was. I could guess. They weren't houses tucked back among the loops of Arrowhead Road, they were mansions, Romanesque, Victorian, modern, Spanish, colonial, God-knew-what, and they all cost around a half million dollars.

"Miss."

"Yes."

"Mr. Oscar is not in his room. Apparently he has not been home this evening."

I waited a moment longer but that was all he said. Oh, Oscar, no wonder you wanted to talk to someone. Doesn't anyone at your house even know where you are at night? Or care?

"Does Oscar not come home often?"

"I'm sure I couldn't say, Miss. And may I ask who is calling?"

Slowly, wearily, I put down the receiver. I leaned against the horseshoe and gently rubbed my temples. The spritzers' glow had evaporated into a dull ache and still in my mind I pictured the sleek midnight blue Maserati. And I knew, knew with a horrible sense of dread, that Oscar had not left his car behind.

I felt a cool eddy of air.

I lifted my head. Behind me, from somewhere behind me, came a waft of cool fresh air. I stayed rigid for a moment then, somehow, forced myself to turn.

Almost directly facing me was the door that led out onto the wooden balcony that overhung the ravine.

The door was ajar. As I watched, it moved. Just a little. Then, in a moment, it swung the other way. Back and forth, in and out, moved by the gentle night breeze.

I walked toward the door. Had it been ajar earlier, when I checked the news-room before locking up?

I didn't remember. If it had been open then, I hadn't noticed it.

I pushed the door wide and stepped out onto the balcony. The wooden floor was slick beneath my feet. Near the centre of the railing, there was something dark. I think I knew, even before I came close and bent down and saw the pale brown tuft hanging on the nailhead. It was a scrap of limp sodden cloth. Light brown cloth.

The Academy requires a uniform. Polished cotton slacks and a camel-coloured sports coat, white shirt and a dark brown tie for boys. Long brown skirts, white blouses and camel-coloured sweaters for the girls.

I leaned over the railing, one arm hugging it tightly, the other swinging the flashlight in slow careful arcs.

He was lying in a crumpled heap about thirty feet below the balcony. He looked oddly small, his head downslope, his hands trailing uselessly behind.

"Oh Oscar . . . Oscar . . ."

It only took the prowl car seven minutes to squeal up to the campus gate. I stood outside the *Herald* office, waiting, my hands jammed into my raincoat pockets, my mouth a thin hard line to hold back the nausea that clawed at my throat.

If I had gone to the *Herald* office when Katie stopped me . . . Of all the sad ifs in my life, this would be the hardest to bear.

I began to wave the flashlight up and down.

The cruiser cut across the parking lot, stopped beside the Maserati and my Rabbit.

"Over here."

They left the light flashing on top of the cruiser and it threw red-and-white flickers across the damp black asphalt and reflected off their shiny black leather jackets.

23

"You the lady that called? A D.O.A.?" He was short, stocky and gruff.

"Yes. This way."

I led them through the *Herald* office and out onto the balcony and, once again, I leaned across the railing, but, this time, I knew where to look.

"Down there."

The two of them leaned over and looked for a moment, then the short, older one said, "Okay, Frank, radio for the meat wagon and the lab guys and Homicide."

"Homicide?" I asked sharply.

"Sudden death, lady. Unexplained."

When the younger man was gone, he said, "Lady, how can we get down there?"

I spread my hands helplessly.

He looked over the edge again, then unsnapped his own flashlight and began to play the beam along the side of the hill. "No damn good way. Well." He ducked back into the office and in a few minutes I saw him, a dark shadow behind his flashlight, beginning to edge his way down the steep incline.

I waited there on the balcony.

The patrolman thrashed his way down the hillside and the bobbing beam of his flashlight came nearer and nearer the crumpled heap that had been Oscar. About five feet from the body, he stopped and the flashlight began to sweep the ground, slowly, thoroughly. Finally he stepped next to Oscar and knelt down but he didn't touch the body. Then, wearily, he stood and looked back up the hillside.

It was almost a half-hour later that Frank came to the edge of the ravine. "The morgue crew's here and Finch and Greeley from Homicide."

"They'll have to wait for the M.E."

Another ten minutes passed and a portly middle-aged man

arrived. I assumed he must be the medical examiner. He too peered over the edge.

I turned and went into the newsroom and slammed the door.

Another half-hour passed. Flickers of light from the ravine drew me back to the balcony. Yet another man was down on the hillside, taking pictures of Oscar from every angle. Finally, two men began to struggle down the hillside with a stretcher. I went back inside. It was another fifteen minutes before a slender, sandy-haired man with a tired face came into the news-room.

"I'm Sergeant Greeley. We've got him up the hill. Would you mind taking a look for us so we can be sure of the ID?"

I was sure, but I had to look for them. It was Oscar, of course, his face white and blanched, wet blond hair plastered to his skull. Oscar had been handsome in a heavy Nordic way. He wasn't handsome now. He was dead.

"Hey, Miss," and the sergeant took me by the elbow as I wavered. "I'm sorry, but we have to know."

"He's . . . he was Oscar Howell II. A student of mine. He lived . . . just a minute, I'll get the address from the school directory."

"93 Arrowhead Road." Sergeant Greeley whistled. "Hey, that house, I know that house. It's the big one. The Spanish castle. Yeah. That's Myra Feldman's house, isn't it?"

I almost whistled myself. I had never made the connection until now. I knew, of course, who Oscar's father was. Even a non-Hollywood type like me knew who Oscar Charles Howell was, the most famous director since George Stevens. I knew Oscar's parents were divorced. Someone had told me that. I never went on to wonder which of Oscar Charles Howell's wives had borne Oscar.

Myra Feldman had been leading lady to every big star of

the fifties. Beautiful and elusive, she had been a recluse for years.

"Myra Feldman's kid! Hey, this is going to be big news. Let's see, Miss, let me have your name? Ann Farrell. Okay. And you live here on the campus? Your number? Okay, okay, that's all we'll need from you now."

He was excited. This wasn't just another stiff.

"Let's see," he was muttering. "I'd better call the chief. And the wire services. And . . ."

He turned back to me. For the first time, he really looked at me.

"Hey, Miss Farrell, how'd you happen to find him? He leave you a note or something?"

I tried to explain, about the Maserati, that Oscar would never have left his car in the lot, and that Oscar had been looking for me at the Herald office.

"But that was hours ago," Greeley objected. "Eight, ten hours ago."

"He wouldn't have left the Maserati," I repeated. "So I knew he had to be on the campus and I was afraid . . ."

"You thought he might jump?"

I hadn't known what to think. But I had been afraid. I frowned. "No," I said slowly. "I didn't think that but I knew he had to be here, somewhere. So I came to the office and the balcony door was open and I found the thread."

"Thread?"

I showed him the little clump of wet thread.

He nodded, then looked at me curiously. "If you were on the kind of terms where the kid was looking for you just before he took a flyer, you must have a pretty good idea why."

"No. No, I don't know why. I would have said that Oscar was the last person in the world to kill himself." I said it and then I realized I believed it. I wouldn't have thought Oscar

26

would do it. Yet, I had been frightened when I found his car. I rubbed my temples. I didn't know what I thought.

"Well, what do you know about him?" the sergeant demanded impatiently.

I knew he smoked a lot of pot. At least until the last week or so. I knew he loved his car. I knew he had a gentle, thoughtful streak. I knew he had lonely eyes.

But I didn't know anything that would explain why he threw himself down a boulder-studded hillside.

THREE

I was dressed and brushing my hair when the phone rang the next morning.

"Miss Farrell?" Dr. Howard demanded, "Why didn't you call me?"

"Call you?"

"Oh my God, yes," he said explosively. "Call me! You find a student's body, and I find out about it on the early morning news. For God's sake, Miss Farrell!"

"Oh." And it was funny. It had never crossed my mind to call him. What did he have to do with Oscar? "I didn't . . . It was so late and I guess I thought the police would tell you."

"I would say you didn't think at all."

I didn't bother to answer.

"I want you in my office at eight o'clock," and he hung up.

Screw you, I thought pleasantly.

I didn't have a class until nine o'clock. Would classes be held? I supposed so.

I pulled my hair back and twisted it into a chignon. I leaned closer to the mirror and began to brush on a coral-coloured lipstick.

The phone rang again.

I snatched up the receiver.

"Ann, I'm so sorry."

"Oh, Dodie." For a moment, tears stung my eyes. "Thank you."

"I'm sorry you were alone when you found him. I wish you had called me."

I took a quick deep breath. "Dodie, he was looking for me. Yesterday afternoon. Katie Bernstein told me. Oh, Dodie, I deliberately went to the coffee-shop. To avoid him."

"Ann, stop it, you mustn't blame yourself. It isn't your fault! You probably couldn't have helped him anyway. Believe me, once someone really determines on suicide, they won't be stopped. I know."

She said it calmly and professionally and confidently. I loved her for it. But she knew as well as I that so many times someone does stop it—and the suicide never tries again.

Could I have saved Oscar?

I couldn't know. Ever.

"If I'd gone to the *Herald* office . . ."

"Likely it would have made no difference. It may already have been over when Katie found you . . ."

For the first time, I began to wonder exactly when Oscar had died. Would the police be able to estimate?

"If anyone should have been alert to something like this, it's me," Dodie said wearily. "Because of Bitsy."

"Bitsy?"

School had been out on Christmas break when Bitsy Martin drowned. She had taken out her sailboat from her parents' beach home at Laguna. It had been a choppy overcast afternoon but for a good sailor it shouldn't have posed any problems. Bitsy Martin had been sailing alone since she was ten. Her sailboat, the mast snapped in half, washed ashore the next day. They didn't find Bitsy's body, or what was left of it, for another week.

"He and Bitsy grew up together," Dodie answered. "They were next-door neighbours. Bitsy always defended Oscar. You know what a stink there was last year. Oh, I guess you

29

wouldn't know, but there was an unholy row by some parents when the Academy didn't kick Oscar out after he was picked up in Hollywood on a marijuana charge. That's one time I really admired Gene. You know what a stuffy ass he can be, but he stood up to them. Gene said kids have to have a second chance. He told them Oscar would be expelled if it happened again but that nobody should be thrown out the first time they made a mistake. Of course, Gene knew and I knew, a lot of us knew, that Oscar was really into pot and the chances of his ever pulling out were slim. But there always is a chance, even when it's angel dust or coke, and, goddammit, if we won't give the kids a chance, hang in with them, who will? And you know something, Ann, this last week or so, I thought maybe Oscar was going to pull out of it."

"I'd noticed it, too, Dodie. He wasn't smoking pot."

Dodie sighed. "I suppose he was really looking at himself and, maybe without Bitsy to buck him up, he just couldn't take what he saw."

"Were he and Bitsy that close?"

"Oh yes. For years. They'd been best friends ever since kindergarten even though Bitsy was so straight." Dodie paused. "I know how Oscar felt. When I heard about her accident, I was just devastated. She was such a marvellous person."

"Do you think Oscar brooded about it and . . . ?"

"It has to be something like that. So you see, Ann, I don't think you could've helped him."

He had tried to find me. He knew that I would understand. Because I had lost someone, too, someone I cared about, and I was still going on, one day at a time. Maybe that's what he had wanted to hear and I hadn't come when he needed me.

"I still feel . . ."

"That doesn't do any good, Ann. Pull yourself together. We've got others to think about today, too. Not just ourselves and Oscar. This is going to be rough on the kids who knew him. You'll be meeting your nine o'clock class?"

"Yes. Of course."

"Let them talk about it, Ann. That's the best way."

The best way for all of us.

The calls had delayed me. I was breathless and five minutes late by the time I reached the ante room to Dr. Howard's office. His secretary sent me right in.

Dr. Howard rose and nodded shortly at me, and two men turned toward me. "Ms. Farrell, may I introduce Lieutenant Fox and Sergeant Petree of the La Villita police department. They are here about Oscar's accident."

But I wasn't really listening. I was responding to a series of stimuli, all of them perceived so quickly they were almost registered subconsciously. Personality is difficult to capture or describe, but some people, men and women, have an air that strikes others immediately. They have a vividness ordinary people lack.

In a news story, you could describe Lieutenant Fox as a man of medium height and build, dark-haired, dark-eyed, thirtyish. In a profile, you could do a little better. Broad-faced with a slightly hooked nose, smooth ruddy brown skin, straight short black hair, eyes as black and impenetrable as summer hot tar, thick-shouldered with muscular arms and thighs and large capable-looking hands.

Lieutenant Fox looked intently at me. "You found the body."

I nodded and explained how.

"I'll want to see the accident scene next," Lieutenant Fox replied. "But, Dr. Howard, before we go, I'd like an announcement made to the school, asking anyone with information helpful to the investigation to meet with me." He paused. "Do you have an empty office I can use?"

"You can use my office," I said quickly. Dr. Howard looked a little irritated at my taking over, then, on second thoughts—and it was just like seeing little balloon pictures in a comic strip—he was pleased. It would certainly keep the police presence unobtrusive.

"That's quite a good idea, Ms. Farrell. We want to cooperate with the police, certainly we do." Dr. Howard sat down and began to rustle some papers. "Although, Lieutenant Fox," and his voice was taking on its faculty-meeting resonance, "I feel Friars' Academy should be disassociated from this unfortunate occurrence as much as possible since it is a fortuity that Oscar fell . . ."

"Or jumped. Or was pushed." Lieutenant Fox said it pleasantly.

Dr. Howard's head jerked up. "There's been no suggestion of anything other than accident. It is certainly unnecessary to speculate . . ."

"I'm paid to speculate."

Dr. Howard took a deep breath. "Of course, officer. We all understand . . ."

The phone on Dr. Howard's desk buzzed. He snatched up the receiver. "Yes . . . yes, Lieutenant Fox is here . . ."

Fox took the phone. "Fox here." He listened for a long moment, his dark face unreadable. "Is Dr. Levy sure? . . . Right. Put the autopsy report on my desk . . . Yes, it certainly does."

When he hung up the phone, Dr. Howard continued full steam, "We'll be glad to cooperate in any way but I would like your assurance that the investigation will be as tactful as possible. After all, Friars' Academy is a well-known institution here in La Villita and I shall be glad to have some of our board

32

members, such as Dr. Fenster and Mayor Cosgrove . . ."

"I'm glad to talk to anybody," Lieutenant Fox said easily. "Especially in a murder investigation."

"Murder?" My voice rose, "Oh, Lieutenant, do you mean it wasn't suicide?"

"No, Miss Farrell. Not possibly."

"Murder! That's ridiculous," Dr. Howard objected. "No one would murder a student here. Not unless there is some kind of madman roaming about. Besides, Oscar was killed by the fall and you can't say . . ."

Lieutenant Fox shook his head. "He was dead on the way down. Or dying. There's a puncture wound beneath his right shoulder blade. A sharp thin rounded piece of metal slid right into the aorta. Dr. Levy said death was almost instantaneous."

"Murder." Dr. Howard's face paled. "That opens up frightful prospects. Murder . . . I must prepare a statement to send home with the students."

Lieutenant Fox gave him a moment to grapple with the shock, then got briskly underway. He wanted Oscar's records, a list of his classes yesterday and the request made that anyone with information to contribute come promptly to the *Herald* office.

Leaving Dr. Howard grim and shaken, we crossed the campus just before the nine o'clock bell rang.

Upstairs in my office, Fox settled behind my desk and pulled a legal pad and ball-point out of his brief-case.

"If you don't mind," but it wasn't really a request, "I'll start with you." He studied me for a moment. "Why were you so glad when I said it couldn't be suicide?"

"Because I would've blamed myself."

"Why?"

I told him then of Oscar's search for me, of my decision to

avoid him and of the empty *Herald* office at four-thirty.

"He was dead by then. Actually, you wouldn't have helped him if you had tried to find him earlier. Didn't you say you decided to go to the coffee-shop just as the rain started?"

"Yes."

"He was dead before it began to rain."

"I didn't know you could determine the time that precisely."

"He was lying face down. His back was drenched but the ground beneath him was dry." He glanced at a pocket notebook. "The rain began at 3:14 P.M."

So Oscar was already dead as I ran up the steps toward the terrace. The dreadful sense of wrongdoing that had haunted me since last night began to lift.

"Can you tell me who disliked him?" Fox asked. "Had he quarrelled with anyone? Sometimes kids can get very angry. Over a girl, money, maybe dope."

I spread my hands helplessly. "If Oscar had an enemy, I didn't know of it."

"All right then, tell me something about Oscar. What was he like? What did he do?"

"Oscar was . . ." I paused. Then I put it baldly. "Most of the time this year Oscar was just a lump, stoned out of his mind."

"Pot?"

"Yes. All fall he sat there at his typewriter, the pupils of eyes like pinpoints, and never moved at all. When he spoke, it was that dull thick voice. You know what I mean."

He knew.

"So, until a couple of weeks ago I couldn't have told you what Oscar was like."

"What happened?"

I shrugged. "Who knows? But, suddenly, Oscar wasn't

high all the time. He was still, oh I don't know how to explain it, wrapped up in himself, abstracted, but, when I said something to him, he responded. Like an ordinary person. And a couple of times, he came into the *Herald* office in the afternoons and fooled around at his typewriter and I think we both knew he was leading up to something. One day in particular he'd started to speak, but the sports editor came in and Oscar turned back to his typewriter "

"Hmmm," Lieutenant Fox said.

"Then once he talked to me about being a reporter. I was with a wire service in San Salvador. He was very kind."

"Kind?"

It hurt all over again. San Salvador didn't mean a thing to Lieutenant Fox.

I turned and walked toward the windows and looked out over the green and brown hillside. "A good friend of mine was killed. Oscar seemed to understand."

"Anything else?"

"I don't know if it means anything, but I remember how it surprised me. A week ago, in Current Events, we got off on the New Morality. Most of the boys were smirky. They think it's pretty grand, you know. Lots of easy sex. The girls are pretty well split on it. Most of them see how they can come out losers. Some of them say, sure, everybody's even, but, of all people, it was Oscar who erupted. His face got red and he said it wasn't fair, persuading a girl it was okay, then, if anything went wrong, she was the one in trouble."

"So Oscar defending fair womanhood surprised you?"

It had. It certainly had. Of all my students, Oscar had been around, in every way. I would have said there was little or nothing Oscar hadn't experienced, seventeen or no. And to have him come out all protective of girls, yes, it certainly had surprised me.

35

"You don't think of anything else? Anything unusual the past few weeks?"

I didn't.

I was getting ready to go downstairs when three sharp buzzes sounded from the announcement speaker. Dr. Howard came on. "Good morning. This is Dr. Howard." A pause. "It is my unhappy duty to inform you of the death of your classmate, Oscar Howell. Further, I must share with you the shocking news, given to me by the La Villita police this morning, that Oscar was murdered." I could hear from downstairs the shocked and subdued exclamations from the classroom where my nine o'clock class awaited me. Dr. Howard continued. "Lieutenant Fox of the Homicide Department will be available in Ms. Farrell's office this morning to interview anyone who feels he has information which might be useful to the investigation. Teachers or students who wish to communicate with Lieutenant Fox are to come to the *Herald* office now. Thank you for your attention."

The speaker system clicked off.

"You can send them up to me one by one, Miss Farrell, if you will."

I was at the top of the stairs when he called, "Oh, Miss Farrell," and he was pointing at my outbox, "These slips, what are they used for?"

I turned to the desk and saw him pick up a square pink slip.

"Those are warning slips," I said easily. "We are required to send them out to a student's parents when a student isn't doing well."

"So students wouldn't have any use for these slips?"

"No."

"At the morgue they pull everything out of a cadaver's pockets. I picked up Oscar's stuff this morning. Had the

36

usual. Car keys. Some change. Pack of cigarettes. A lighter. But there was one unusual thing."

"Yes?"

He waved the warning slip. "A fresh pad of these. Would you have any idea, Miss Farrell, why Oscar would have had an unused pad of teacher's warning slips in his pocket?"

I stared at the paper in his hand. The all-capital heading, OFFICIAL WARNING, was so clear and black and distinct.

FOUR

"Pink slips," I said steadily, staring at the pad in Lieutenant Fox's hand. Did my face change? I don't know, but he sensed something out of the way.

His black eyes watched me intently. "Yes, Miss Farrell. Pink slips just like this one."

I shrugged. "I can't imagine what Oscar would want with them."

Oscar writing me a poison-pen note? Oh no, I didn't believe it. Wouldn't believe it. The Oscar I was beginning to know, that Oscar wouldn't have written me a hateful letter.

"You're sure it doesn't mean anything to you?"

"Sure." I answered too quickly. He knew the pad meant something to me. Too many years of asking questions had instilled a fine-tuned antenna. He looked at me for a long moment, then his eyes dropped to my desk.

I was terribly aware of the waste-basket so near us, just half a foot from him, and the uneven mound of crumpled papers in it. It hadn't been emptied last night. Damn the clean-up crew. Why had they missed my waste-basket last night?

I could see the wad of pink paper on the very top.

"Lieutenant." I moved closer to him and leaned across the desk to pull out the shallow centre drawer. As I'd hoped, he half-turned to watch me. My left hand dropped out of sight beside the desk. "There are pencils and papers here. And over there," I pointed across the room, "there is some instant

38

coffee and cups. I just use hot water from that basin." My left hand closed around the wad. As I began to straighten up, I slammed the centre drawer shut with my right hand. I was shoving my left hand into my skirt pocket when he caught my wrist.

"I'll take that."

We stood frozen for a moment, his hand firm around my wrist. He didn't force my fist open. It was up to me, but I knew that if I refused he could arrest me as a material witness and take me to the police station to be searched by a matron. I remembered what small-town jails looked like from a summer I spent on a suburban paper, covering the police beat.

I opened my hand and the pink wad fell onto the desk-top.

"Thank you." He used a couple of car keys to spread the pink slip open. It didn't take him long to read, then he looked up at me. "Not a welcome message, I should think."

"No."

"If you'd like to obtain counsel, Miss Farrell, you may."

I was breathless for a moment, then I said sharply, "I don't need a lawyer."

He looked at me, then down at the note. "You and a married man?"

There was just a shade of disappointment in his voice and it was absurd how that hurt.

"I didn't . . ." I stopped, my face flushing. "Oh, hell."

"You didn't what?" He poked the note with a car key. "Are you saying this isn't true?"

"Not exactly."

"That what happened at the Calavetti Motel?"

Could I explain the Calavetti Motel? Would anyone ever understand it? Did I understand it myself?

I walked away from him to look out across the ravine. The

39

morning fog, thin and gauzy, had almost burned away and the steep, green-spangled hillside glistened. I could see Sergeant Petree and two other men working their way slowly back and forth down the ravine toward the crumpled spot where Oscar had landed, dead or dying from a stab wound in his back.

That trampled spot and the palm trees in San Salvador and the blue-and-yellow tile floor of the San Merino Room in the Calavetti Motel all mingled in my mind.

I told him then about Michael and my return to the United States and Friars' Academy . . . and Clay.

"Clay is . . . well, you'll meet him when you talk to Oscar's teachers. Clay is . . . attractive." That was how I put it because how do you tell a man about another man? That the way he moves attracts women as surely as the spinning wheel lures a gambler? That he has thick blond hair and eyes that crinkle when he smiles and a bold, infectious laugh? A very attractive man. "He was terribly nice to me, this fall." And I was hungry for someone to care. All alone and hungry. "Somehow we always seemed to end up alone together." That first week-end in November, we were working as faculty sponsors on Kismet and we bumped into each other backstage between the thick heavy folds of the curtain, and, abruptly, we were in each other's arms and his mouth was hard and demanding against mine. It was the next week, when we were out on Thanksgiving break, that Clay called and invited me out to dinner. "We went to the San Merino Room at the Calavetti Motel." It was a leisurely meal and all the while he looked at me and there was no disguising his intent. It was like being swept up on a wave, going faster and faster, and never counting when it would break. After dinner, we danced and then, it was almost eleven. "I have a room," he said easily. "Would you like to have a nightcap?" The wave arched higher. "We were walking across the foyer, toward the elevators, when a middle-aged couple came out of the bar. Clay pulled me behind a huge leafy plant." It was a couple he knew, friends of his and June's. He tugged on my arm and nodded toward the back stairway. Hole-and-corner, that was the phrase that popped into my mind. I shook my head. He looked a little surprised, then he shrugged and smiled pleasantly and drove me home. We had been on the best of impersonal terms ever since.

I turned and faced Lieutenant Fox. "I changed my mind." I didn't try to explain why.

He nodded. "But it would be awkward to have it brought up with Dr. Howard?"

"Yes."

He nodded. "A note like this could cause you some trouble but someone else may have received a note they would go to any lengths to keep private."

"Someone else?"

Fox's bright dark eyes touched mine. "Poison-pen letters usually come in bunches, Miss Farrell. Not singly."

Oscar writing poison-pen letters. Oscar? "I don't believe it. I just don't."

"Why not?"

"Oscar wasn't that interested in other people. He was . . . Well, of course, most of the time, he was just too stoned to pay any attention to anybody. And lately, even though he's been alert, he hasn't been keyed into people. He was all wrapped up in something inside himself."

"But you don't have any concrete reason to believe someone else wrote the note?"

"No."

"When you first saw it, who did you think might have written it?"

I shrugged. "I had no idea. None. I was so shocked by it.

41

Then I got mad. Then I thought to hell with it and went out to dinner."

"Hmm."

If he chalked that outburst up to bravado, he didn't let on. Instead, his eyes, those dark intent eyes, glanced down at his notebook then back to me.

"Right, Miss Farrell. Now, if you can tell me where you were between two and four o'clock."

I looked at him in surprise.

"Between two and four o'clock," he prodded.

"But I couldn't have killed Oscar."

"Why not?"

Whoever had stabbed Oscar had then hefted him over a three and a half-foot railing. Oscar was almost six feet tall. He must have weighed at least 180 pounds. I'm five three and can just manage to stash a couple of the LA phone books on a head-high shelf in the news-room.

"Look at me . . ." I began.

He did, and, for an instant, I lost track of my argument. Then, my face hot, I explained.

He nodded. "I don't believe you could have thrown him over the railing . . . by yourself."

I started to tell him angrily that Clay and I had not conspired to kill Oscar, but I knew Lieutenant Fox would only nod and say, "Right," so I answered him.

"I was in the Library from just after two until about three. Then I walked toward the Administration Building. That's when Katie told me Oscar had been looking for me. I almost went to the *Herald* office, then I decided I didn't want to see Oscar so I went up the steps to the terrace."

"Did anyone see you in the Library?"

"I don't think so," I said slowly.

He waited.

"I was using a study carrel, one of the soundproof ones along the back corridor."

"No one came up and down that corridor the hour you were there?"

"I was working. I didn't pay any attention."

"Right." Then, briskly, "Thanks very much, Miss Farrell," but his eyes weren't brisk, they were speculative. "Now, if you'll send those coming to be interviewed upstairs, one by one, I would appreciate it."

I was starting down the circular stairs when he added, "And, Miss Farrell, if you should discover anyone else who received a poison-pen note, let me know."

It was a disjointed day. I have no idea what I said to my classes. I'm sure they didn't remember either. It was altogether too distracting as people came to be interviewed. Every time someone rounded the corner into the news-room, I jumped up to welcome them and explained softly that Lieutenant Fox was upstairs and they should take a seat until he called down for the next person to be sent up.

I didn't write down the names of those who came. I didn't need to. I could remember. Katie Bernstein and the teachers Oscar had Thursday, Jennifer Prince for English, Clay Fredericks for history, Pat Porter for drama, Alice Calhoun for chemistry. All of them nodded gravely at me except Pat Porter who came over and whispered nervously, "Look, Ann, I'm not involved in this at all but Howard sent a note saying all his teachers should come. Why? I don't know anything. What's this cop like?"

"Oh, he's very nice, Pat."

Pat tugged nervously at his tartan vest. He was really in a sweat and he didn't even look as spectacular as usual. Pat was using the Academy as a way-stop while he tried to break into the movies. He was just a shade more handsome and athletic

43

than thousands of good-looking beach boys hoping for elevation via celluloid. Pat had become engaged over Christmas to the daughter of the well-known director, Carlos Contreras. She was pudgy-faced, dumpy and lisped. I hoped stardom would be worth it.

I had a free hour at eleven. By then there were only two left to be interviewed, Dodie Wingate and Jason Horvath, a student. I had never had Jason in class but I knew him by sight, a tall weedy boy with severe acne who always wore mirrored sun-glasses. As he waited, his face occasionally turned toward me but, of course, I couldn't tell whether he was looking at me or the wall behind me or nothing at all.

I kept wondering what Lieutenant Fox was learning and whether anyone else had admitted receiving a poison-pen note. It occurred to me that Belinda Bascomb and Paul Casteel were likely candidates.

Should I tell Lieutenant Fox about Belinda's outburst at the faculty meeting? And Paul's uncharacteristic behaviour when he came into the coffee-shop? That would have been shortly after Oscar was murdered. In a way, didn't Paul's odd behaviour almost clear him? If he had just killed Oscar, wouldn't he have been sure to act as normally as possible?

Murder is an awful act, especially if not committed in a drugged or violent state. If Paul had killed, he had done it deliberately. Wouldn't there follow a period of shock and strain? If he had shoved a knife through a sports coat, felt the resistance of flesh, heard the involuntary gasp of pain, mightn't he very well have looked grim and strained?

What should I tell Lieutenant Fox? If Belinda and Paul weren't involved, I didn't want to cause them trouble.

Alice Calhoun stepped around the curve. "Next."

Jason Horvath looked at Dodie. "You can go ahead, Mrs. Wingate."

44

"That's all right, Jason. You go on."

Jason nodded and ambled slowly out.

Dodie looked after him. "Jason was Oscar's best friend."

"He's not in any hurry."

"No," Dodie said absently. She snapped open her purse and pulled out her cigarette case. I don't permit smoking in my classroom, but, for once, I kept my mouth shut. Dodie lit a cigarette, drew on it nervously. "Ann, I can't decide what to do."

"Tell the truth and shame the devil."

She shot me a quick look. "I wish it were that easy."

"Oh."

"Right. The truth's going to be awkward."

"Why?"

She took a deep drag on the cigarette. "I was searching Belinda Bascomb's desk when Oscar was killed."

I'm not often at a loss for words but it conjured up such an incredible picture. "My God, why?"

She threw the cigarette down, stubbed it out on the flagstoned floor. "I think she's the bitch who is writing the anonymous letters. Oh, you wouldn't know about them, but there has been a rash of really ugly letters. I'm just sure Belinda's behind them. I mean, who else is hysterical and repressed? It takes a neurotic like Belinda to slaver around about other people's sex lives."

I was trying to cut in, say I'd had a letter, too, but Dodie was talking hard and fast. "If I'd found any proof, I was going to shake her until her neck cracked like a chicken's. I was . . ." Dodie broke off, breathing heavily, her face red. "I could just kill her!"

"Dodie, look, you can't pay any attention to scurrilous stuff. And nobody really cares. You know that."

"Seth cares. It would . . . Oh God, I'd rather die than have Seth find out."

I had met Dodie's husband several times and liked him a lot. His good humour matched hers and, at a party, you could hear his booming laugh over the cocktail roar. I admired him. You have to admire a man in a wheelchair who can always greet you with a smile. Especially a man late come to a wheelchair. He had been career Army, a captain in Vietnam when a land-mine exploded just under the jeep in front of his. His jeep was thrown to the side and he came out of it alive but with a broken back.

Yes, I imagined a certain kind of note, if it were true, would be very tough for Seth Wingate to handle.

"It was just . . . just a temporary madness. You know . . ." She looked at me, shook her head. "No, you don't know. You're too young to understand. And it isn't . . . I mean, Seth's all right, you know," she said awkwardly. "It isn't that at all. I think it was just a . . . just a romantic thing." She paused, looked unseeingly toward the balcony windows. "God, I must have lost my mind! And Seth wouldn't understand. He would think . . . And it wouldn't be that at all. He's a hundred times more a man than Clay. Oh God, I don't even like Clay."

But I scarcely heard the last of it. Clay. Oh my Lord, he must be the Lloyd George of Southern California. What a fool I had almost been.

I don't know why it incensed me so. Not at Dodie, of course. Because of Dodie. Dear, plump, unadorned, kind Dodie. For Clay to go after me, well, that was part of the game. I was old enough to know what I was getting into, but single. No trauma. Dodie . . . I was looking at her, trying to, from a man's point of view. Another woman can never do that, really. Her slightly blowsy figure and dowdy clothes might mask an overpowering appeal. Even so, Clay played poker with Seth Wingate once a month. He knew the man.

They were, casually at least, friends. Not very attractive of Clay.

". . . got to stop those notes!"

But the notes had been stopped if Lieutenant Fox was right and Oscar wrote them.

I asked, "Why do you think Belinda's writing them?"

"You saw her at the faculty meeting."

I nodded.

"It's obvious she's under a terrible strain," Dodie continued. "She's close to a breakdown and I'm sure the notes are why. She's been writing them and she's afraid someone will find out. It's typical hysterical response."

"Maybe it's because she's received a note herself."

"Oh, she's too repressed to have done anything to bring on that kind of note."

I wasn't sure Dodie was right on that. Although, God love us all, surely she hadn't been another of Clay's conquests. Then I was ashamed of myself. Not very attractive of me.

"Anyway, Belinda doesn't matter now. I'll deal with her later. What am I going to tell that detective?"

"As much of the truth as possible."

"My God, Ann, I can't . . ."

"Hold on. I don't mean bare your bosom. Just tell him you wanted to talk to Belinda about the spring rummage sale and you waited outside her office but she never did come."

Dodie thought it over. "I guess so. Sure. That sounds okay." She sighed, pulled out another cigarette. "Thanks, Ann. I don't know why it seemed so impossible. I suppose I'm not thinking too straight. That'll work and . . ."

Jason Horvath poked his head around the corner. "The lieutenant's ready for you, Mrs. Wingate."

After Dodie went upstairs, I wandered uneasily around the news-room. Lieutenant Fox would be finished with Dodie in a few minutes and, if he came down, I didn't want to see him. Not knowing what I did about Dodie. I had a feeling he would know I was keeping something back.

Once outside, shrugging into my white sweater, I hesitated at the top of the *Herald* steps. Then, with a decisive nod, I set off for the Fine Arts Building.

FIVE

Belinda's eleven o'clock class was almost over. She stood near the kiln, wearing a baby-blue smock. "Careful now, Lyle. Open the door slowly. Very slowly."

I waited in the hall. The students began to stream out, moving quickly. It was time for lunch and those with off-campus privileges were hurrying for the parking lot and freedom for an hour.

Belinda was in a hurry, too. She darted out of the classroom, pulling on a spring coat, baby-blue, of course, and looking eagerly down the hall. I was behind her.

"Belinda."

She jerked around. "Ann?" She was both startled and wary.

"I'm so glad I caught you. Let's go to lunch."

"Lunch." She repeated it like a word in a foreign language.

"The Pink Cabbage is good. I just love their spinach quiche. Or, if you'd like a drink, how about Little Tony's?"

Unless she wanted to be outright rude, she was trapped. "All right," she said finally. "I guess I can."

When we came to the swaying foot-bridge that led to McDonough Hall and the lot where I kept my car, she balked. "I didn't even know this was here. Do you cross it every day?"

"Sure."

She clung to the weathered stanchion and peered into the ravine. "It makes me dizzy to look!"

49

I refrained from suggesting she not look. "Oh come on, Belinda. It isn't far, really."

She looked at the other side and it wasn't far. No more than fifteen feet. "Well, okay."

We weren't even halfway when she stopped, closed her eyes and grabbed at me, both hands grasping like claws. "It moves," she moaned piteously. "It moves!"

Of course it moved. It was a suspension bridge.

She stood, her eyes squeezed shut, and she began to waver.

"Come on, Belinda, this way. I have you. I won't let you fall. That's good. One step. Another. That's great, we're almost there."

By the time we reached the other side, sweat was streaming down my face and sides and Belinda was trembling and pasty-faced.

She opened her eyes and gasped for breath. "I'm sorry," she stuttered, "awfully sorry, Ann."

"That's all right."

Once at the car, I decided on Little Tony's. A drink with lunch sounded great. We got a booth at the back and settled against the hard wood with a joint sigh. We sat in an awkward silence until our Bloody Marys came. Belinda took a big gulp, then demanded, "Why did you ask me out to lunch?"

I took a big gulp, too. I was wrung out so I didn't try to be tactful or clever.

"It's the pink warning slips. You know what I mean. The ones . . ."

Her face flushed. Her mouth opened. But no words came. Instead, tears began to stream down her face, running in rivulets through her make-up.

"Does Dr. Howard know?" she wailed.

I shook my head. Good grief, was Dodie right? Had

Belinda written those notes?

"Oh Ann," she moaned, "what am I going to do?"

I felt awkward and awful. Why had I decided to poke and pry? I didn't care who'd written the damn things.

"Oh Ann," she cried again, "what if Mother finds out? And she will if I lose my job." She fumbled in her shoulder bag for Kleenex and began to dab at her face.

"He won't fire you," I said feebly. "If you told him you didn't mean to write the notes . . ."

Her head snapped up. "I didn't write the awful things."

So Belinda was a recipient. I looked at her with new interest. What could Belinda have done to provoke an anonymous letter?

"If Dr. Howard finds out . . ."

"It can't be that bad, Belinda."

"It wasn't bad. It was wonderful. I've never felt that way before. And that week-end in San Francisco . . . I didn't think anyone would ever find out."

I looked down at the table. I didn't want to watch Belinda's face.

". . . I've never loved anyone else . . ."

I wished I were a million miles away. I felt tawdry. Clay was certainly a first-class rat.

Belinda said even more softly, "I don't care what happens. Vicky and I . . ."

I drew my breath in sharply. Vicky! Oh good grief. Belinda was right. She would be booted off the campus before sundown if Dr. Howard found out. And so would Vicky, the assistant girls' PE coach new to the campus this fall. Lesbianism might be *au courant* in the SF bistros, but baby, it hadn't come any way at all on a private school campus.

". . . should just quit."

"Oh no, Belinda, don't do that."

She looked up at me and, slowly, I could see it happening, she began to wonder how I knew. And what I intended to do.

"Ann, how did you know?"

"I didn't know for sure."

Her plump hand darted across the table, caught my wrist. "What gave us away? Tell me!"

I pulled my hand free. Belinda in tears was depressing. Belinda aggressively defending herself was distasteful.

"Nothing, really. But you got so upset at the faculty meeting . . ."

Belinda grimaced. "Vicky told me I shouldn't have let it upset me so. I thought he was talking about us, in the art lounge."

I didn't want to hear the intimate details. "But you had already received one of the pink notices, hadn't you?"

"Yes." Her eyes narrowed. "How do you know about them?"

"I got one." Her eyes lighted up at that. It might not be fair but I wasn't going to tell all. "And Lieutenant Fox is trying to find out who else has had one."

"Why?" Belinda asked sharply. "Why does he want to know?"

"He thinks Oscar wrote them."

"Oscar?" Either she was a marvellous actress or the idea had never occurred to her. "Why, how in the world could Oscar have known?"

I didn't drive back to McDonough Hall after lunch. I thought it would be asking too much of Belinda to cross the rope-bridge twice. Instead, I pulled into the Academy's main entrance and dropped her off by the Fine Arts Building, then turned into the faculty lot west of the Administration Building. I heard the first bell ring but I didn't get out of my car. I needed to hurry if I was going to meet my one o'clock class on time but I made no move to open the door. Instead I watched Paul Casteel walking toward Mellaert Hall where his maths classes met. As he disappeared inside, I jumped out and called to Jimmy Simon, who was in my one o'clock Current Events class.

"Jimmy, I'm going to be a little late to class so everyone is to write an essay on this week's cover topic in *TIME* magazine."

"Okay, Ms. Farrell."

The last stragglers were disappearing into classrooms as I went up the stairs in Mellaert Hall. I knocked on Paul's office door.

"Come in."

His office was oppressive. A huge African warrior's shield dominated the wall behind him. The top of his book-case, every inch of it, was covered with gleaming dark wooden sculptures. A mask, daubed with bright red and yellow paints, dangled from a wire attached to the ceiling.

He waved me to a seat. "Do you like my little lair?" he asked, his voice high and lazy.

"It's different."

"I like different things. Different experiences."

I looked around the office again. The silence expanded. "Have you been to Africa?" I asked finally.

"Oh yes. Twice." He began to smile. It wasn't an especially nice smile. "If you like these things, you must come to my apartment sometime."

Again, that difficult, uncomfortable silence. "Paul, I was wondering . . ."

He tilted his head toward me like an interested parrot. "Yes, Ann. What were you wondering?"

I had blundered directly into success with Belinda. Would it work twice?

"The pink notes, Paul. I've come to see you about the pink poison-pen notes."

His pale-blue eyes bored into mine. "What do you know about them, dear?"

"A little," I said cautiously. "And the police-lieutenant, the one investigating Oscar's death, asked me if I knew of anyone else who had received one. He thinks Oscar wrote them."

"Anyone else?" Paul repeated. He began to smile. "Isn't that sweet. You're looking for company. Well, I'm sorry, darling, I really can't help you out."

Paul was not Belinda. He wasn't going to ante.

I decided to make it more interesting for him. "There was a list of people in Oscar's pocket. When he was killed."

That wiped the smile off Paul's face. "A list?"

"Your name is on it." If I was going to lie, I might as well do it with a flair.

I had Paul's attention now, but he only said, "So?"

"Lieutenant Fox is sure he'll find some evidence among Oscar's things as to what the notes were about."

I saw Paul's shoulders relax. Implicit in what I said was the admission that the police had no idea now what had been in the notes. Paul lifted the lid of a cigarette-case and took out a long pale green cigarette. "So Oscar wrote them. That surprises me." He lit the cigarette and a plume of lime-scented smoke drifted aross the desk. "Looks like Oscar made a mistake."

"What do you mean?"

He shrugged, inhaled deeply and I wondered if his lungs were green.

"Oscar's dead. Maybe he learned something. Like, minding his own business." Those pale-blue eyes clung to mine.

54

I was pushing back my chair when he asked, his voice amused and malicious, "I'll tell you what was in my note, Ann, if you'll tell me what was in yours."

The sound of his laughter, soft and high, followed me out into the hall.

Go right ahead and laugh, I thought. I wasn't yet finished with Paul. He couldn't treat Lieutenant Fox quite so lightly. But I was thwarted. When I returned to the *Herald* Building, my office was dark and empty. I spent the remainder of the hour grading the essays and wondering why Paul had received a note.

If Oscar had written Paul a poison-pen note and if the accusation had not only been true but a secret that Paul could not permit to become public, Paul might well have killed him.

Where had Paul been yesterday between two and four? And where was Belinda? She wasn't in her office because Dodie had searched it.

I gave up all pretence of work and walked slowly around the classroom. It had been this time yesterday afternoon when Katie had dropped by and Oscar was here and they talked. I must have missed Oscar by only a few minutes. I had left the news-room directly when class ended and gone to the library. If I had stayed, I would know now what Oscar had wanted of me.

I stopped and stared at Oscar's place, the third typewriter in the back row. I could picture him sitting there, his bulky shoulders dwarfing the flimsy back of his straight chair, his shaggy blond hair drooping across his face, making him toss his head every so often, his huge hands moving clumsily over the keys.

I had read his copy, watched him in class, accepted the tentative beginnings of friendship . . . and I didn't have a single idea why he had wanted so badly to see me yesterday.

Did he need help? Was he afraid?

I shook my head at that. Quickly. Oscar had not been afraid. Even at the last moment, when death stood behind him, I was sure Oscar had not been afraid.

Oscar had been angry.

But not, surely, at me.

That brought me back to that note, that hostile angry note to Ms. Farrell. HUSSY. Oscar wouldn't have known that word. There were other words Oscar knew. But why would he apply any of them to me? Why would Oscar care where I spent my nights? Or with whom. In fact, if I'd thought about it at all, I would have guessed that Oscar would have said, "Have at it, Ms. Farrell."

Besides, why would Oscar have been so anxious to see me if he was going to drop a poison-pen note on my desk?

It didn't make any sense.

Life often doesn't make sense and there was that packet of pink notes in Oscar's pocket when he died.

I frowned and walked down the aisle and stopped beside Oscar's typewriter.

Why had Oscar wanted to see me?

I stared at the unresponsive keys of his typewriter. If I only knew what he had been thinking yesterday. Yesterday he sat there. I knew it because the typewriter was humming when I came to the *Herald* office at five o'clock to lock up. I had reached down and clicked it off . . .

I stared at the typewriter, not humming now, and at its empty carriage and I felt a prickle down my back. The carriage had not been empty yesterday afternoon. There had been a half-filled sheet of yellow copy paper. I had glanced at it and noticed just enough to think that Oscar had been fooling around, the typewriter equivalent of doodles. Just a string of words, some underlined, a series of question marks and exclamation points and capitalized words.

Where was that sheet of paper now? Who had pulled it out of the carriage?

The typewriters sat on wooden stands with a single shallow front drawer. I yanked open Oscar's drawer.

I should have known. Of course, I should have known. Another pad of pink slips and a sheet of copy-paper with a typed list of names. I pulled the drawer out until I could read the entire list.

Funny. I had tried to frighten Paul Casteel with an imaginary list. Here was as nice a list as anyone could desire. My name was third.

DODIE WINGATE
CLAY FREDERICKS
ANN FARRELL
PAUL CASTEEL
BELINDA BASCOMB
JENNIFER PRINCE
PAT PORTER

I took a pencil from the drawer and delicately shifted around the pink pad and the loose sheet of paper. There was no half-filled sheet of yellow copy paper. I looked thoughtfully at the empty carriage then at the floor. I had gathered up some wads of copy-paper this morning after Dodie went upstairs. I crossed to the waste-basket and dumped its contents onto the horseshoe. I unwadded every ball and there was nothing that looked like the sheet I had glimpsed in Oscar's typewriter.

I was positive the sheet had been in the typewriter late yesterday afternoon when I went upstairs. It was then that I had found the pink notice on my desk. It was only a little later that I heard the downstairs door open and someone had gone into the news-room.

Who had come in downstairs?

Was it the murderer, returning to get that sheet from Oscar's typewriter . . . and perhaps to put that nice list of suspects in Oscar's drawer?

What if Oscar hadn't written those notes at all? What if instead he had discovered the identity of the writer?

Would the writer murder to hide his authorship?

Well, that was as reasonable as to assume that Oscar had written anonymous letters to a handful of people who could scarcely have mattered a damn to him. Oscar wasn't an ordinary teenager. All right. I'd buy that. He was different. For one thing, he was very, very rich and that makes anybody different. But he wasn't frustrated or a weirdo or, I would have bet, sexually maladjusted. He wasn't the kind of person to hide behind a poison pen.

But, on the other hand, face it, he wasn't the kind of person to give a damn about who wrote the letters. He might even think they were funny.

"Oh hell." I shoved the scraps back into the wastebasket.

Why would anyone kill Oscar? That was still the main question. Obviously, it was more dangerous to the murderer to have Oscar live than to kill him, despite the risks that entailed. There had to be a compelling, overriding, urgent reason.

How could a kid like Oscar pose that kind of threat to anybody?

That brought me back in a circle to the poison-pen letters. I walked slowly to Oscar's typewriter and looked down at the list of names. Oscar's list of poison-pen pals? That, of course, is what it looked to be. And I would have to call Lieutenant Fox and tell him that I'd found it. I shoved the drawer shut. I didn't believe any of it but Lieutenant Fox would look at me with his somber dark eyes and say, reasonably enough,

"Look, Ms. Farrell, you don't have any facts to indicate someone else wrote the notes . . ."

I could tell him until my tongue gave out that Oscar never wrote poison-pen letters, and he would only nod non-committally and start interviewing everybody on the list. I hoped he would see Dodie at school and not at home.

I called the police department and finally had to settle for leaving a message.

Then I leaned against the horseshoe and tried to re-member what I had seen on the paper in Oscar's typewriter yesterday.

***** ????? FIX FIX FIX *WITNESS*

Lots of exclamation points, too. Only two words, fix and witness. Fix. Pictures of some sort? Repair? To get even? Drugs? To pay off? That might tie in with witness. Or could it be eyewitness? And what could Oscar have to do with fixing a witness? I tried to block out everything but the memory of that moment when my eyes swept casually across the paper.

Witness and a string of $ signs.

I gave it up finally. It must have meant something to Oscar. I shivered. And to his murderer. What would have happened if I had called out when the door opened late yes-terday afternoon?

Would someone I knew have walked up my curving stairs, smiling?

It would have been someone I knew. Only Dr. Howard clung to his delusion that a deranged stranger had stabbed Oscar and dumped him off the balcony.

If I knew more about Oscar, those tag end remnants of the thoughts he had the day he was to die might make sense. Sense enough to trap his killer. If I knew more about Oscar . . .

SIX

The houses were so far back from the road that it was almost like driving in a wilderness, only an occasional glimpse of a high chimney or bright swath of red tiles betraying their presence. I almost missed the turnoff, the only sign two small gilt numbers on the roadside mailbox. I made the turn and dipped instantly into a feathery green tunnel as the narrow road bored between pepper trees. The road curled like a serpent through the lush semitropical shrubs and trees. The sweet smell of honeysuckle drifted in the car window. The road ended in a gravelled semicircle in front of the house. I parked the Rabbit inconspicuously at the edge of the turnaround and looked up at the house. And up and up. Twenty rooms. Thirty. Forty. It was immense, a Hollywood dream of Alhambra, stuccoed and tiled like a rococo wedding cake.

It was absolutely quiet. The turnaround was empty, except for my Rabbit. In my experience, death brings a flurry of activity. There is a subdued intensity. The silence daunted me and the looming, grandiose immensity of the house. I stood uncertainly before the huge door. It was at least twelve feet tall, a rich dark rosewood, intricately carved, with blue tiles inset in the panels. A golden bell pull hung from the mouth of a lion's head near the lintel. Slowly I reached up and tugged.

The door opened noiselessly. Instead of a dark cavernous

interior, the entrance hall was bathed in golden sunlight from a light well and the blue tiles of the door were repeated in the floor of the entryway.

The butler had pink cheeks and a balding pink skull and a clipped English accent.

"Miss?"

And what in the world did I say now? How could I expect to gain access to this house?

"I'm Ann Farrell. From Friars' Academy. I found Oscar."

"Oh yes, Miss. Do you . . . ?" He paused, uncertain himself how to proceed.

"I thought perhaps Oscar's mother would like . . . I could tell her what happened."

"Oh yes, of course, Miss." He hesitated, then said briskly, "If you will come this way, Miss, I will inquire whether the mistress can see you."

I followed him down the long hall past a magnificent stone stairway that rose in a slow curve to our left. He opened a double set of doors and stood aside for me to enter. He touched a switch and wall sconces glimmered to life around the perimeter of the most magnificent room I had ever seen outside of a French chateau.

It was a full twenty minutes before she came, walking regally, one hand just lifting the long sweep of her red velvet hostess gown. For an instant, as she came through the door, I was stunned by her beauty, the perfection of line from cheekbone to chin. Just as beautiful as ever, I thought, and, as she came nearer, I felt a swift rush of disappointment. The puffy ridges beneath her eyes, the sharply indented lines at the corners of her mouth, the thick caky make-up to hide raddled skin. And it wasn't the ravages of grief. No, this was more insidious, a product of years, not hours.

I would have liked her better had her eyes been reddened,

but they looked at me, slightly hazy and fuddled, though clear of tears.

"Miss . . ." she paused. "Jenkins said you are one of Oscar's teachers." Her voice was incurious, remote, repeating slowly and carefully what it had been told.

"Yes. I had Oscar in editing class this fall. I found him last night and I thought you might want to hear how it came about, Mrs. Howell."

"Oh no, no," she said quickly, and I was afraid I had, after all, touched a nerve. "Oh no, Miss . . ."

"Farrell."

"Miss Farrell, I am Myra Feldman. Miss Feldman. The other was long ago and far away."

"Oh." I took a breath. "Miss Feldman."

She looked at me attentively. "You were saying . . ."

"I thought you might want to know how I found Oscar."

"It was late at night." She spoke every word so slowly, so distinctly.

"Yes. I'd been out to dinner. It was almost eleven when I got back to the campus. When I drove in the main entrance, I passed the student lot and that's when I saw Oscar's Maserati and I knew he wouldn't have left it . . ."

I stopped finally and it was, for a long moment, utterly quiet in the huge, opulent room.

She blinked and looked at me blindly. "One of Oscar's teachers . . . ?"

"I thought you might know if Oscar had been . . ." I looked at her aging but still lovely face with the wide-spaced dull eyes, "worried about anything lately. Or upset."

"Worried?" Her brows, those perfectly formed brows, arched together in a slight frown. "Why, I don't think Oscar ever worried about anything. He was a quiet child. Always. When I saw him last, oh, it must have been one day last week, why, he was just as usual."

Oh, Oscar. One day last week. That was the last time she saw you. When was the last time she ever thought of you?

She brushed one hand against her face. "Of course, it's been difficult."

"Oh, I know," I said quickly, "and I'm sorry to bother you . . ."

She went right on, not even hearing me. "Very difficult. Because someone in my position," and she smiled archly at me, "why, it wouldn't do to have a grown child about. I mean, the public doesn't expect it! And really, that was when everything started to go wrong, when Oscar was born. I missed the role of Melinda in *The River Dies*. You remember that film, don't you? It won six Academy Awards. One of them should have been mine. If I hadn't been pregnant, I know I would have had the role. That made me quite ill, you know, and the directors stopped thinking of me. Oh, it can happen to easily, so quickly. The young ones think it never will happen to them, but they just don't know. And all because of Oscar."

I stared at her. Oh Oscar, dammit, how could I have missed seeing the ache in your heart?

"You hadn't seen Oscar this week?"

She shook her head. "I've been so busy . . ."

"Do you know any of his friends? Anyone who might have some idea why this should have happened?"

"Friends," she repeated vaguely. "I don't know, really. Oscar was free to bring his friends home, and, of course, he had his own apartment, really a lovely area of the house. It was all his own. Perhaps Mrs. Jenkins would know who visited Oscar. She is the cook but Oscar formed quite an attachment to her. Would you like to talk to her?"

"Why yes, if you wouldn't mind."

"Of course not." She smiled graciously. "I would like to do all I can for one of Oscar's teachers."

She rang for Jenkins. We waited without speaking.

The double doors opened.

"Madame?"

"Jenkins, Miss . . . uh . . . this young lady is one of Oscar's teachers and she wants to talk to Mrs. Jenkins. About Oscar's friends."

His well-trained servant's face remained expressionless but I saw the quick little intake of breath. He waited just an instant long to reply.

"Certainly, Madame." He looked at me intently. "This way, please, Miss." He nodded toward an inconspicuous door beneath the staircase. It opened onto a narrow flight of stairs that led down to an immense kitchen. "Miss, if you'll wait a moment, I'll see if Mrs. Jenkins can talk to you."

I stood beside the butcher's block and tried to hear the low-voiced exchange in the next room.

"There's a young lady here. One of Mr. Oscar's teachers. And she wants to talk to you."

"To me? And why should that be?"

"She wants to know about Mr. Oscar's friends. Perhaps she's helping the police."

"Then don't keep her waiting, Henry. Of course, I'll see her."

When he took me into the little room, she pulled herself heavily to her feet from a worn rocker. I held out my hand. After a moment's hesitation, she took it.

"It's awfully good of you to see me, Mrs. Jenkins."

She tried to smile at me but couldn't. Her face was pale and drawn, her eyes red from weeping, and I knew someone grieved for Oscar.

"I'm sorry," I said gently.

Tears flooded her eyes. Her mouth trembled.

"Now, Mother," Jenkins said quickly. "Please, Mother."

She held her apron to her face for a long moment. Her voice was muffled. "Oh, it didn't ought to have happened. He never hurt anyone, not Mr. Oscar. Why would anyone kill him? Why?"

"That's what I'm trying to find out." For the first time I recognized what I was doing, why I was here. It didn't ought to have happened!

She patted the apron against her face, then let it fall. "Are you with the police?"

"No, I'm one of Oscar's teachers. I'm . . ."

"You must be Miss Farrell, of course. That's who you are."

"How did you . . . ?"

She smiled. "Oh, Mr. Oscar's talked to me about you. Many's the time. He thought you were so pretty."

For an instant, tears stung my eyes. Oscar had liked me. I knew that. Then, like a sliver of ice, I remembered. HUSSY. Two faces to Oscar? Love and hate?

"I'm glad Oscar thought I was pretty. He was one of my most interesting students." Especially, I thought, the last few weeks when he wasn't stoned all the time. She was nodding proudly, so like a parent that I felt stricken. How often at parents' evening had I made an innocuous comment to a parent who would take it and ramble happily, delighted to attribute all kinds of marvellous qualities to John or Susie with scarcely any help from the teacher.

Mrs. Jenkins was nodding and talking, rapidly, happily, "Ah yes, Mr. Oscar, he was a quick one. And he always was, right from the beginning when he was only a little tyke. Why, he could talk a blue streak when he was only two. He would

65

come to my kitchen, that was always his favourite place, and stack up my pots and pans and chatter faster than any magpie. When he was only seven, he learned the Morse code! Would you believe that, Miss! Just a seven-year-old boy."

Colour flooded her face. Jenkins watched her protectively, sadly, and we both listened to her snatches of memory, Oscar as a Cub Scout, Oscar and his tenth birthday party, and hadn't that been a wonderful day. She'd fixed his favourite chocolate swirl cake, and there had been monkeys from the zoo, his daddy had seen to that, and even She'd been gay and beautiful, and Mr. Oscar was so happy. That was the happiest day.

"The happiest day." She repeated it quietly and her eyes clouded. Then, defensively, almost argumentatively, she pleaded for him. "He had a hard life. Yes, a hard life. People wouldn't think so, to look at this house, to hear of his school and the places he'd been, the advantages he'd had. But he was such a lonely little boy. No one to care. No one but us and sometimes she'd take him away for months, go to a health spa and take him along, just a little boy, and no one to care for him. He'd be so thin when they came back and he would stay for hours in the kitchen, his great blue eyes just watching me. Oh, I tell you, Miss, no one will ever know how hard it was for Mr. Oscar. Just us and Miss Bitsy to care for him. Miss Bitsy, she was a lovely one and she meant so much to Mr. Oscar. They are together now and perhaps that's what was meant to be. Mr. Oscar and Miss Bitsy together again."

Behind her, all one wall was full of pictures of Oscar. An angelic little blond boy in a sailor suit, his eyes wide and trusting. Grinning in his Cub Scout uniform. Serious in a class picture. But there were not many recent pictures.

She followed my glance. The tears began to stream down her face again. "Oh, I drove him away. When it all started."

I knew she meant the drug use.

"Mother," Mr. Jenkins said quickly. "Don't blame yourself. You were trying to help him."

"But I wouldn't let him come and see me when he wasn't himself. And, finally, oh, he hadn't come in such a long time. Until the last few weeks." Again her mouth trembled. "It was almost like it used to be, these last few weeks . . . except Mr. Oscar was so unhappy about Miss Bitsy. But he was himself, his eyes clear and bright. You know what beautiful eyes he had, Miss."

"Yes." Blue eyes dark as northern lake water. "That's what I want to talk to you about, Mrs. Jenkins. The last few weeks. Something happened to Oscar these last few weeks and I think it must have something to do with his murder. That makes sense to me. So, if you have any idea what Oscar was thinking about and what he was doing these last few weeks, it may help us find his killer."

She nodded slowly. I could tell that she hadn't, until now, thought past the fact of Oscar's death. She hadn't begun to wonder why. Until this moment, the enormity of his murder had overshadowed any thought of why.

"The last few weeks? Well, that's easy, Miss, easy and so sad. It was all Miss Bitsy. At first I thought he'd grieve himself sick but then he got mad." She frowned. "I know that sounds funny but it's true. He was mad, mad as hops. I'd find him in his room, late at night, just sitting there staring at a picture of Miss Bitsy and his face would be so hard and his eyes wild, just wild."

We were quiet for a moment and I could almost sense Oscar near us, as if he were standing by Mrs. Jenkins, and I could feel an echo of his anger, a terrible consuming anger.

Why was Oscar so angry? Angry at God or Fate or the coldly impersonal ocean? Anger made no sense. I could understand grief and sorrow and pain. But rage?

Anger. Anger at someone? Could he blame a person for Bitsy's death. But that made no sense either. It was an accident, a senseless, useless sailing accident.

"You don't think of anything else?"

Mrs. Jenkins shook her head. "That I don't, Miss."

All right. She was part of Oscar's life, had been a big part before pot enveloped him. But there had to be others who would know more what Oscar had done these last few years and especially these last few weeks.

"Who were Oscar's friends? Who came to see him?"

They came and went, most of them nameless to Mrs. Jenkins. There were only a few who had been Oscar's friends for any length of time. Bitsy, of course, and Jason Horvath, and, once or twice, but not recently, Ian Campbell.

The last surprised me. Ian was one of the golden ones, good-looking, fun, popular, outstanding both in academics and sports. I wouldn't have thought he would have much in common with Oscar, stoned or not.

I was thanking them for their help when Mrs. Jenkins asked if I would like to see Oscar's room.

"It's just the way he left it when he went to school yesterday morning."

Oscar must have left his room without any sense of finality. He couldn't have known this would be his last morning to hurry down the stairs to his Maserati and slip beneath the wheel and feel the surging power beneath him as the car roared down the canyon road. He couldn't have known.

But he must have been set on a course that was leading him to that balcony.

What was Oscar thinking yesterday morning? Yesterday afternoon, he had sat at his typewriter and punched out FIX and WITNESS and a series of $$$$$$. Would there be anything in his room to explain those words?

Mrs. Jenkins led the way to another set of back stairs that led up to his suite on the second floor. She bustled ahead to open the door.

It was a long lovely room done in tones of beige and brown and a dusty gold. There was a huge stereo complex along one wall. Another wall was covered, almost every inch of it, with photographs mounted on mats.

She was proud of them. "Mr. Oscar took all those pictures himself. I always thought he would grow up to be a director like his father. Aren't they beautiful? His dark-room is just past there."

Oscar had never indicated any interest in photography at school. But I could see that he had had real talent. The pictures were balanced with an uncanny sense of lighting, the sea at sunset, redwoods in the morning mist, a peach tree bursting with ripening fruit, the spume of breakers crashing over jagged rocks. And Bitsy. Picture after picture. There was an empty space at the centre of the wall where a large photograph had hung. I looked around the room. The picture was lying on a coffee-table beside an easy chair. Almost reluctantly, I walked closer to look down at it.

It was a marvellously lifelike photograph of Bitsy standing on the deck of a sailboat, her face half-turned toward the camera, surprise and laughter in her eyes, the wind ruffling her short blond hair and moulding her shorts and T-shirt against her. A summer picture. A happy picture.

I looked at the chair. It still showed the impress of Oscar's body. He had sat there, holding the picture in his big powerful hands.

Bitsy. Everything led to Bitsy.

SEVEN

I could see the tennis court from the circular drive in front of the house. It was green plexipave with a rose apron. Wisteria, thick with purplish blooms, covered the end fences. As I watched, the woman in the near court served. It was a good serve, hard, flat and angled wide to the receiver's forehand. The girl on the far court stretched, managing a short forehand in return. The server was coming in. She had a putaway volley but she turned her racket face down and the ball went in the net.

I hesitated. I could go up the front steps, ring the bell and ask for Mrs. Martin, but I knew I was watching her as she picked up the balls and walked back to serve from the far back court. I could see her so well. Her hair was short like Bitsy's but flecked with grey. Her face was flushed with exertion but she was smiling. She was not, at this moment, thinking of Bitsy. It couldn't help but make her unhappy to talk to me.

Everything led to Bitsy. It was Bitsy who had dominated Oscar's last days. Still, did I want to barge in and speak my piece and watch the happiness drain out of Mrs. Martin's face?

I was turning away when I heard the shout. "Hello. Hello. We're down here."

I swung around and waved and, after an instant, began to walk down the grassy green slope toward the court.

They were standing by the net, waiting. I smiled. "Mrs.

70

Martin? I'm Ann Farrell. I teach at Friars' Academy and . . ."

Her eyes widened a little. Abruptly, she looked much older, but still so much like Bitsy. If Bitsy had lived, she would have matured like this woman with a clear fine complexion and little laugh lines splaying out from her mouth and eyes.

". . . I wanted very much to talk to you."

"I'm sorry," the girl said abruptly and for the first time I looked at her. She didn't resemble her mother or Bitsy. She was tall and slim with long black hair worn in a single thick braid. Normally she would be pretty in an aristocratic way. Now she stood, her head jutting forward, white patches at either end of her mouth, her face determined. "Mother can't talk to you now . . ."

"Mickey!"

There was no ignoring the command in her mother's voice. "Mother, please, we don't want to . . ."

"We don't want to do . . . what?" Mrs. Martin reached out, gently touched Mickey on the arm. "What's wrong, Mickey? Why, we don't even know why Miss Farrell has come." She looked at me inquiringly.

If I could have dropped into a hole, I would have. I could feel Mickey's eyes burning at me. I knew, for whatever satisfaction that it brought, that I was right. There was something odd here. Something odd as hell. Bitsy and Oscar. But this lovely older woman standing here, looking at me with trusting pain-filled eyes, didn't know about it. Whatever it was, she didn't know. And Mickey did.

"I've come about Oscar."

"Oh," she said sombrely. "I heard. On the radio. I'm so terribly sorry. I was afraid he might do something like this."

I realized then that they didn't yet know it was murder. It would surely be in the afternoon news-papers and on the upcoming broadcasts so there was no reason for me not to tell them.

Mrs. Martin listened with shock and horror. I shot a quick glance at Mickey. She was frowning, her dark eyes intent.

"Oh, how awful!" Mrs. Martin exclaimed. "Why would anyone kill Oscar? Oh, that's dreadful!" Mrs. Martin looked at me gravely. "Is that why you've come? To talk to us about Oscar? But why? What could we know that would help explain Oscar's murder?"

Your daughter knows, I thought. I didn't look at Mickey, but I didn't need to. She stood tautly, her face white and still, scarcely breathing as she waiting for me to answer.

"Everyone has told me," I said tentatively, "that Oscar was terribly upset at Bitsy's accident. Upset and angry."

Mickey drew her breath in sharply, but Mrs. Martin was standing a little in front of her daughter and she was watching me, caught up in what I was saying.

Mrs. Martin nodded. "Yes." She sighed. "Oscar loved Bitsy very much. We all loved Bitsy," her voice broke a little, "but sometimes I thought Oscar cared more for her than anyone. It used to worry me." She shook her head. "Oh God, if that's all I had to worry about now." She pressed her lips together, "But that couldn't have anything to do with Oscar's murder." She looked at me sharply. "You aren't thinking . . . ? Well, it sounds so melodramatic! You can't be thinking that someone killed Bitsy and then Oscar! It couldn't be, Miss Farrell. Tell her, Mickey."

Mickey looked at me, her eyes dark with fury and something more and I thought it might be fear.

"Tell what?"

"About the day . . . Bitsy had her accident."

"There isn't anything to tell. It's all in the papers if Miss

Farrell wants to read about it."

"Mickey!"

The girl grimaced then spoke quickly, harshly, her voice clipped and angry. "It was Sunday morning. Everyone had gone to Mass except Bitsy and me. She had been to the early service. And I was sick."

Sick. No. For whatever reason she had stayed at the beachfront home, it wasn't because she was sick.

She glared at me.

"If I had stayed at home . . ." Mrs. Martin began and the anguish in her voice was agonizing.

"Oh, Mother no, no, it wouldn't have made any difference."

"It might have."

"But she so often went out to sail. You know that. It was just an awful accident. You can't help accidents."

Mrs. Martin looked down at the ground. "No," she said heavily, "you can't help accidents."

Mickey was watching me tensely.

"You saw Bitsy leave?" I asked.

She nodded, never taking her eyes away from mine. Why? Was she trying to foresee my next move?

"She was alone?"

"Yes."

"What do you think happened?" I asked suddenly.

"I think she must have been sunbathing," Mickey said rapidly, glibly, "and a swell caught her by surprise and she slipped off."

"But she was such a good swimmer," Mrs. Martin objected. "I don't understand why she couldn't have caught the boat. You know how Bitsy could swim."

"I know, Mother, but anyone can have a cramp. And she didn't have on a life-jacket."

"That's all wrong, too," Mrs. Martin said forcefully. "She always wore her life-jacket."

"Well, one time she didn't. And it was the wrong time."

Mrs. Martin nodded wearily. "She had promised me . . ." Suddenly her face crumpled and she began to cry. She help up a tennis towel. "Oh, I'm sorry, Miss Farrell. Sorry. I thought I could . . ."

"Go on up to the house, Mother. I'll talk to Miss Farrell."

Mrs. Martin turned blindly and began to walk, so slowly and tiredly, up the crushed-shell path.

When she was out of earshot, Mickey turned on me. "Leave us alone."

"You know more than you're telling."

"Damn you," she said softly. "Don't you see what happened? It's so obvious. And if you keep talking to Mother, then one of these days it will come to her. Now she's grieving. If she knew, it would destroy her."

"Knew what?"

"Bitsy committed suicide."

It was like watching the shifting, colourful bits of a kaleidoscope slowly settle into a pattern. Bitsy was an expert sailor, a superb swimmer, young, healthy, strong. How could it have happened? It was so obvious when you looked the right way at the facts.

Still, how could her sister be so sure.

"How do you . . . ?"

"You can't tell Mother!"

"I wouldn't do that."

"It doesn't have anything to do with Oscar. He knew, of course. He and I."

"But how?"

"She left a note for him and one for me. I took it to him. After the funeral." Her face was drawn and bleak. "It was

74

awful. I've never seen anyone cry like that. I used to tease Bits, you know, about her faithful dog Oscar. Oh God, it was awful. Worse even than for Mother and Daddy because . . . I don't know, but they are old, you know, and they know everyone is going to die and they felt that an accident like that happening to someone like Bitsy had to be meant somehow. And they have such faith . . . and that's why they mustn't ever know it was suicide. It would just kill Mother. She feels now that Bitsy's in heaven and if she knew it was suicide . . . ! Oh, they just can't know!" She reached out, touched my arm. "So please, please go away. Don't talk to Mother again. Please."

"Mickey, believe me, I don't want to hurt your mother. I don't want to and I won't. But I think Bitsy's death has something to do with Oscar's murder. It's all tied up together. Oscar goes along for years, stoned out of his mind, then, your sister dies, and, all of a sudden, he stops using dope and starts stalking around in a fury . . . then he gets killed. It can't just be coincidence."

She frowned. "It doesn't make any sense, Miss Farrell. It was Oscar who was killed, not the man who . . ."

She broke off but she didn't need to finish her sentence. It had already occurred to me why a girl like Bitsy might take out her sailboat never intending to return.

"Was she pregnant?"

Mickey nodded miserably.

"Do you know who . . . ?"

"No. I don't even have an idea. She wasn't dating any of the boys she used to go out with." Mickey paused, then said wearily, "I'm afraid she was involved with a married man."

"Bitsy!" It shocked me. I hadn't known her except by sight, but what I knew of her made that kind of situation seem so unlikely.

Mickey nodded. "Last November she said something to me about how dumb boys her age were and how much more comfortable she felt with older men. I was a little surprised because I didn't know of any older guy she was going out with so I asked her who and she just smiled and said somebody I knew and he was a lot older but he had told her how mature she was. I didn't like the sound of it so I asked if he was married. She got all defensive and said you couldn't always look at things a certain way. I snapped back like a self-righteous prig and said a married man was a married man and she'd better remember that!" Mickey grimaced. "If I had just kept my mouth shut! She told me to mind my own business and slammed out of the room."

"I wouldn't have thought Bitsy would even consider slipping around with a married man." I pushed away the uncomfortable thought that I knew someone else who had almost slipped around with a married man.

Mickey sighed. "I wouldn't have thought so either. But, don't you know, he probably said he was separated, something like that. And she was just a kid."

But when she turned up pregnant . . . ?

"In her note, she only said that he couldn't marry her and she couldn't tell Mother and Dad." Her mouth twisted bitterly. "If Bitsy hadn't been such a nice girl . . . did you know her, Miss Farrell?"

I nodded. Not well but I knew who she was and she always smiled and said good morning when we passed. A nice girl. Not the kind of girl to know how to handle that kind of trauma. Pregnant, unable to marry, barred from abortion. Young and scared and frightened and heartsick.

"She was too sweet," her sister said. "Hell, I have two friends who have had abortions. Water off ducks. Another one just had the kid and works and drops her off at the nursery and goes on dates like it was the most normal thing in the world. But Bitsy didn't know anything about living like that. She couldn't face telling Mom and Dad. It must have seemed impossible to her. If only she had told me. I knew something was wrong. That's why I stayed home from church that morning. I was going to talk to her. I heard her come in from the early service so I started breakfast. I had it planned, you know, a leisurely visit over breakfast. When I went up to her room to call her, I saw her dress lying on the bed. I started looking for her and I heard the door to the boathouse open. It has a high squeak. I ran but by the time I got down the path to the beach, I could just see her sailboat curving out of sight around the headland. I shouted but she didn't hear me." She looked at me forlornly. "If I'd hurried a little faster."

When her sister didn't return and the search began, Mickey had found the two notes tucked into her purse. She'd read the sad, scratchily written note addressed to her.

"It was already too late by then." She looked at me defiantly. "I read my note then I burned it. I decided that Mother and Daddy shouldn't know. Not ever. Why make it worse?"

I nodded.

"So you see, what happened to Bitsy doesn't have anything to do with Oscar."

"If Oscar knew who the man was, if he threatened to expose him . . ."

Mickey was shaking her head. "Oscar wouldn't have done that. He knew Bitsy didn't want Mother and Dad to know. He would have done anything to keep it quiet. For Bitsy's sake. And he promised me he would never tell anyone."

But Oscar had been grieving and angry. I understood now what caused the tortured look in his eyes. What if he had brooded and decided, finally, that somehow the man should pay?

But it was Oscar who was killed. And he wasn't killed in self-defence. He was caught unaware, stabbed from behind.

"Did Oscar know who the man was?"

"I don't know," Mickey said slowly. "I didn't, of course, read the note to him. I mean, my God, I wouldn't do that! It was in an envelope with his name on the outside. So I don't know what Bitsy wrote to him." She frowned in thought. "She may have told him. She told Oscar a lot of things. But what could Oscar do if he knew? Don't you see, he wouldn't tell anyone because that would be making Bitsy's name cheap. He wouldn't do that."

"If Oscar threatened to tell the man's wife . . ."

"So what?" Mickey responded. "He could lie to his wife. Anyway, big deal. Would a guy kill Oscar just to keep his wife from learning about an affair that could never be proved?"

She was anxious for me to see how unlikely it was. She wanted it to be unlikely. She didn't want anything to focus attention on Bitsy . . . and her accident.

"Look at it," Mickey insisted. "This isn't the Dark Ages or anything. Nobody's going to commit murder to hide an affair."

"It doesn't seem too likely," I agreed, and I was ashamed of her obvious relief. She even looked at me with a degree of friendliness.

But I wondered. How about a man who could not afford the scandal of having driven a teenage girl to suicide?

Who was he? A name and face came to me. Oh, surely not.

Mickey was talking, ". . . see that whatever happened to Oscar, it doesn't have anything to do with Bitsy?"

"Well," I temporized, "you would think that if it hinged on Bitsy, we would be charging Oscar with murder instead of looking for his murderer."

"Right," she said quickly, approvingly. Then, looking up

the hill, she caught her breath. "Oh, Miss Farrell, here comes Mother. You won't tell her? Please, you won't . . ."

"No, don't worry. There's no need. None at all."

I refused an offer to come up to the house for tea and thanked Mrs. Martin and Mickey for their help. As I drove away, I hoped there never would be a need to have anyone learn the truth about Bitsy's death. And especially not her parents.

But I was going to find the man, and, deep in my mind, I already knew whom I suspected.

EIGHT

At the foot of the canyon road, I hesitated, then turned up the narrow blacktop leading to the Academy. I had to go lock up the *Herald* office. I parked and walked fast, not liking the emptiness of the campus.

It had been just about this time yesterday that I'd turned off Oscar's typewriter. Now he was at the morgue, lying on a movable metal slab with an ID tag tied to the big toe on his right foot.

I gritted my teeth and hurried into the news-room. Then I stopped and stared at Oscar's typewriter. Unwillingly, I reached down and opened the desk drawer. The pad of pink slips and the list of names still lay there.

I knew what I had to do.

This time the operator put me through to Lieutenant Fox. He said he would come immediately, and he did.

He didn't touch the drawer-pull. Instead, he jostled the desk and when the drawer opened a bit, he levered it out using pencils at either end. When the sheet with the list of names was visible, he paused and read it, his dark face impassive.

"Don't you think," I was going to make a try, "that the list is a little fortuitous?"

He looked up at me from under dark straight brows. "Fortuitous?"

"I mean, how awfully handy. And I didn't think to tell you

earlier about the person who came into the *Herald* office late yesterday afternoon."

"Who?"

"I didn't see anyone but I heard the door. You know what a distinctive sound it makes. It was just after I'd found the pink slip on my desk. As you can understand, I wasn't in the mood to talk to anybody. Anyway, I heard the door open and someone went into the news-room and just a few minutes later came out again and left."

"So?"

"The sheet of paper in Oscar's typewriter was taken out by someone. Maybe the same person put the pink slips and the list in the drawer."

"But that would mean Oscar didn't write the pink slips," Lieutenant Fox objected. "And we don't have any reason to think that."

"Oh, yes we do," I said stubbornly. "I keep telling you, Oscar wasn't the kind of kid to write poison-pen letters."

"Oscar hadn't been himself these last few weeks. Everyone I've talked to has told me that."

"But now I know why." I was eager now. My words tumbled over themselves as I told him what I had found out from Mrs. Jenkins and from Bitsy Martin's sister.

He heard me out then shrugged. "That only confirms what everyone's said. Oscar was upset. He wasn't himself. And the notes make sense then. He was getting back at everyone. The people he looked at, they were still alive and Bitsy wasn't. Grief takes people like that sometimes."

I tried again. "Oscar was angry! And he was angry at the man who drove Bitsy to suicide. Look at it that way for a moment. Maybe Oscar threatened him and the man decided to murder Oscar but to make it look like someone else did it, he wrote the notes and sent them, then, after he had killed

Oscar, he planted the pink-slip pad on him."

"If it was so well planned, why didn't the murderer put the second pink pad and the list of names in Oscar's typewriter drawer then? Why wait an hour or so and come back to do it?"

I shrugged. "Maybe he didn't remember until later that Oscar had been sitting at his typewriter. Maybe when he remembered the sheet of paper in the carriage, he knew he'd better get it and he decided to put in the second pink pad and list to incriminate Oscar?"

He looked at me kindly enough. "I appreciate that the people on that list are your friends. I understand that it's always easier to imagine some shadowy super murderer than to believe someone we know can kill. But, believe me, murder is usually just as simple as you can make it. Sick and ugly, but simple. Oscar was upset about his girl friend's death, yes, everybody says so. But his grief took a twisted turn. He was a twisted kid. But, unfortunately for him, he pushed the wrong button." He looked down at the list. "One of these people had a secret they had to keep."

We both looked at the list.

DODIE WINGATE

CLAY FREDERICKS

ANN FARRELL

PAUL CASTEEL

BELINDA BASCOMB

JENNIFER PRINCE

PAT PORTER

"You can help me," he said suddenly.

"How?"

"You know them. They're your friends. Tell me why they are on that list."

Dodie. Sweet, funny, desperate Dodie.

"Lieutenant, I can't. At least, I can't talk about some of them."

"I'm not in the business of judging people's morals, Miss Farrell. I'm looking for a killer. Someone who shoved a narrow sharp piece of metal into a boy's back."

I didn't answer.

"Look," he said gently, "just tell me what you can."

So I didn't tell him about Dodie. I guess, after I'd finished and she was the only one I didn't mention, that he knew who I was protecting. He was quite interested in Belinda. Of course, I didn't know what Paul was hiding.

"I couldn't even guess about Paul, but he scares me. And nothing would surprise me. As for Jennifer, I think she has a fondness for young men. In singles bars. I suppose if a big fuss were made about it, it might cost her her job. Pat Porter? Who knows? I've never heard anything against him. He's engaged to Carlos Contreras' daughter. Pat's very ambitious and he's auditioning for a part in Contreras' new movie."

Pat Porter. Handsome Pat. It would be easy for a girl to fall in love with his tousled blond hair and sleepy blue eyes and perfect profile. Had Bitsy been in any of his classes? I would find out.

"This gives us a lot to work on." He looked around the room. "I'll take this drawer into the lab. I'll give you a receipt for it."

I took it. Then, abruptly, I asked, "Lieutenant, about that list."

"Yes?"

"Will you do me one favour?"

"If I can."

"Please don't go out to Dodie's house to talk to her. Have her meet you here at school."

He hesitated an instant, then nodded. "All right. I'll do that."

He picked up the drawer, protecting its sides with copy-paper. I went ahead of him down the passageway and held open the heavy front door. He waited while I locked up then we crossed to his car. He put the drawer in the boot. When he slammed it down, we stood for a moment and there was an awkward silence.

I thrust out my hand. "Good night, Lieutenant."

When I drove the Rabbit out of the lot, he was still standing on the deserted stretch of asphalt, looking after me. His figure diminished in my rearview mirror, was gone, but his presence stayed with me, sturdy, substantial, rugged.

He was a complex man. A determined man. He would follow wherever that list led him. He felt sure one of those names belonged to a murderer.

I shifted down to low, eased the Rabbit onto the bridge that crossed the ravine.

He knew about crime and that was his judgment. Maybe he was right.

Maybe.

The car bumped off the bridge and I turned to my left toward the McDonough Hall Parking Lot.

Maybe he was right.

But I wanted to know who the man was, the shadowy faceless figure behind a sailboat bucketing out into open ocean, never to return.

NINE

"Hello?" Her voice was Saturday-morning sleepy.

"Katie, this is Ann Farrell. I'm sorry to call so early, but I wanted to ask you something."

"Sure, Ms. Farrell," she said fuzzily. "What can I do for you?"

"Who was Bitsy Martin's best friend?"

There was a long pause and I could picture Katie Bernstein waking up, beginning to think. "Best friend," she repeated thoughtfully. "Well, I'm not positive, Ms. Farrell, but I think Shannon Kirk is who you want. She's a senior. Tall, red-headed. Do you know her?"

"Oh yes, I know who she is. Thanks, Katie."

"Sure, Ms. Farrell."

I thumbed through the student directory and called Shannon's number. She didn't live far from the Martins.

"I'm sorry," a cheerful voice replied. "Shannon's gone for the day."

"Do you know where I could reach her?"

"Oh, she's out of pocket. Bobby Phillips picked her up about an hour ago. They're going to spend the day working on his boat. He keeps it at Marina del Rey." She paused, "If it's terribly important, I suppose you could try the marina office but . . ."

"Oh, that's all right. It will keep."

I rinsed my breakfast dishes, showered, pulled on levis and

a lemon-coloured turtleneck. I had lots to do today, plenty of plans. And I was supposed to meet Bill Abshier at the Racquet Club at two. I liked Bill. He was pleasant and cheerful. We would have a fun set or two then settle on the verandah and drink margaritas. A pleasant man, a pleasant afternoon. But all the while, I would, I knew suddenly, be thinking of two other men. One a shadowy unknown figure, the other clear and distinct in my mind. The first man was, I was sure, a handsome man, a sexually exciting man with a taste for youth. He might not, perhaps, be especially young himself. What had attracted Bitsy to him? Charm and sophistication and the cachet of capturing the attention of someone far out of the ambit of boys her own age? Unwillingly, two faces came to mind. I could see Clay's lazy sensual charming smile and Pat's tousled good looks. The other man in my mind was very different from anyone I'd ever known. Different and fascinating. Fascinating because he was so different? I liked the smooth ruddy colour of his skin, the deep blackness of his eyes. It would take years to learn to read his eyes.

And that, of course, brought Oscar to mind and my Saturday plans seemed unimportant. I didn't want his murderer to get away with it and I felt, rationally or not, that I was the only one who could really find out what had happened.

Marina del Rey was one of the loveliest pleasure-boat anchorages along the coast.

I took Santa Monica Boulevard to the San Diego Freeway, travelled south on it then exited onto Venice. A weak sun tried to shine through the smog, but it only made the sky look fuzzy and out of focus. Despite the car fumes, I could smell the moist ocean air and glimpse an occasional palm.

I went to the marina office first. A dour old man grudgingly checked his register then he yanked a thumb over this shoulder.

"His boat's the *J. P. Vanilla*. The last pier."

Midway down the pier, I saw Shannon. She was on her knees, sanding the port side of the cabin. Her vivid red hair hung loose. She wore a floppy yellow sweat shirt and white pants and white sneakers. She didn't look up as I walked closer. Neither did the young man coming out of the cabin. They weren't expecting company.

"Shannon."

She looked up. She was like so many red-heads with a thin translucent skin that made her appear delicate and vulnerable. Her blue eyes widened in surprise, then she smiled and began to scramble to her feet. "Hello, Ms. Farrell. How are you?"

"Fine." There was a short awkward pause. "Shannon, I'm sorry to bother you but I need to talk to you for a moment."

The surprise was deeper now. "To me?"

"Yes. You knew Bitsy Martin well, didn't you?"

She drew her breath in with a quick little gasp. The young man looked at her. He began to scowl at me.

"Bitsy's dead," Shannon said faintly.

"But you know why, don't you?"

Unwillingly, she nodded. "How do you know?"

"Mickey told me."

Some of the tenseness seeped out of her body. If Mickey had told me, it must be all right. But she was still wary.

"I don't see any point in talking about it."

"If you don't want to talk about it, you don't have to," the boy interrupted. He turned toward me, "I don't know who you are, but it's time for you to split." He slipped an arm around Shannon. "Come on, we'll take her out."

"Shannon, please talk to me," I called. "I have to know who the man was. I think he murdered Oscar Howell."

The boy turned back toward me. "Murder. Lady, what the

hell are you talking about?"

He let me come aboard then and I told them what I thought. Shannon listened intently.

"Have you told all this to the police?" he asked finally.

I nodded.

"So, if it's such a big deal, why haven't they talked to Shannon?"

"They're looking at some other possibilities." I didn't want to talk about the pink slips.

Shannon was staring down at the water, her face sombre. Then, haltingly, she began to speak. "Bitsy asked me to go to Laguna with her family that weekend. I didn't want to, Bobby, because you were going to be home." Her eyes filled with tears. "If I had gone, maybe she wouldn't have . . . We had talked about it, about her being pregnant, a couple of days before and I thought I had convinced her to tell her folks. I mean," and she looked at me imploringly, "her folks . . . it would have been hard because they loved her so much but they wouldn't . . . I mean, it wouldn't have been so bad. She could have gone away, had the baby, put it up for adoption. I thought I had persuaded her. I never thought . . . I never thought . . ." she hid her face in her hands and her shoulders shook as she cried.

He pulled her into his arms and glowered at me. "Get out of here. Leave Shannon alone. None of this is her fault. You're just a damn busybody. If the cops want to talk to Shannon, well, that's all right. But she doesn't have to talk to you."

No, she didn't have to talk to me. Nobody did. Maybe everybody thought I was a busybody. But if Shannon regretted not going to Laguna that weekend, I regretted the impulse that had turned me toward the coffee-shop and away from the *Herald* office, away from Oscar.

And I wasn't going to stop or be deflected until I had done my best to find out what really happened and why.

I didn't stay at the marina to watch the *J. P. Vanilla* pull out.

I sat in the Rabbit for a long moment. For the first time, I felt uncertain. Maybe I was wrong. Maybe no one else saw what I did because there was nothing there to be seen. Maybe it was just the way it appeared. Oscar had written anonymous letters and they had been the death of him. That's what Lieutenant Fox thought.

But I didn't think Oscar had written them. If Oscar didn't write them, who did?

A twisted angry person? Or a cool calculating killer?

Was Oscar killed because he discovered the identity of the poison-pen author or were the poison-pen notes written to give a plausible reason for Oscar's murder?

I knew what I believed.

The Oscar I knew wouldn't have written the notes but he also wouldn't have given a damn about them. If he'd known who had written them, he wouldn't have cared.

Oscar had had other things on his mind these last weeks.

But, if the notes were written to provide a reason for Oscar's death, it told a lot about the writer. It told that the crime was premeditated and it told that the killer knew a great deal about Friars' Academy and its faculty.

A very great deal. Enough to know the hard-kept secrets of a half dozen people. Enough to know how isolated the *Herald* office was. Enough to know that I often worked at the Library during my afternoon off-hours.

I started the Rabbit up with a roar, jolted out onto the street and turned back toward La Villita.

I wasn't having comfortable thoughts. All along, of course, I had accepted, almost automatically, the thought that the killer must be part of the campus, someone I knew. I had even looked at those who received the pink notes with that kind of scrutiny, wondering if any one of them could be desperate enough to protect themselves from exposure by knifing Oscar.

This was another kind of thought altogether. This was assuming a clear unemotional logical plan to dispose of a problem and it brought to mind a cold, wilful arrogance. It also brought to mind the faces of the men I knew on the faculty because, if the killer had been Bitsy's lover and, at the same time, so incredibly knowledgeable about the well-kept secrets of the faculty members, then he almost had to be on the faculty himself.

There were about thirty faculty members and about half were men. I knew all of them. Some of them could be dismissed from consideration out of hand. Not Dr. Howard. I didn't know, of course, what he would like in the way of sex but I knew enough, was close enough in age to Bitsy, to be absolutely sure he would have no appeal to her whatsoever. Zilch. It didn't take long to sift through the rest of them. It came down to three. Pat Porter, Steve Tibbets and Clay Fredericks.

But which one?

Three men. All of them attractive. But only one of them, Clay, was married.

Did I really think that Clay, who liked life to be easy and pleasant, was the kind of man to knife a boy in the back?

Or Pat? Or Steve?

Three men. How could I hope to discover which one had been involved with Bitsy?

Maybe I should leave it all up to Lieutenant Fox. He was capable and smart and he knew a lot more about murder than I did.

I knew a lot about Friars' Academy.

I swung into the Academy road. Maybe I should give it up. After all, I hadn't done too well with Shannon. I was curving past the Administration Building when I saw Dodie's shabby yellow Chevy. On impulse, I swung into the lot, parked next to her car and hurried in the side door.

It was eerily quiet, the way buildings are at odd hours. Dodie's office was on the second floor toward the back. Halfway down the corridor, I almost turned back because there was no light shining through her frosted glass. But I had come this far. Maybe it would be unlocked. I might see if I could find the filing-cabinet with the personnel folders.

I knocked perfunctorily then turned the knob. The door wasn't locked. I opened it and stopped short.

Dodie sat slumped behind her desk, staring at nothing. She looked old and shrunken.

"Dodie, what's wrong?"

She stared at me as if we were strangers.

"Dodie, what is it?"

"I'm so afraid." She spoke so softly I could scarcely hear.

I came around the desk, put my arm around her bowed shoulders. "Tell me what's happened."

"He's going to arrest me! If he does, Seth will find out." She looked up at me with wild eyes. "I'll kill myself, I swear it."

"Dodie, listen to me, don't say things like that." Even as I heard my own words, I realized how utterly stupid and useless they were. "Dodie," I almost yelled, "he isn't going to arrest you."

Hope flared in her eyes then died away. "Oh yes, he is," she said dully. "He knows the pink slip must hide something awful because I begged him not to ask Seth about it. But I know he will. Today or tomorrow or the next day. And then

91

Seth will ask me. And I shall kill myself."

"Dodie, look at me. Look at me, dammit!"

She just stared at the desk-top.

"Dodie, I think I know who killed Oscar."

Slowly, her face reformed, came to life. She reached up, grabbed my arm. "My God, Ann, who?"

"The man who made Bitsy Martin pregnant."

She understood almost at once. Bitsy and Oscar and his unrelenting anger.

"Who?"

"One of three men, Dodie," and I told her who.

She considered it in silence for a long moment. "But why just those three? Oh, I can understand why you don't put Howard on the list or some of the others, but why narrow it to three men on the faculty?"

"The pink slips, Dodie. What if Oscar didn't write them? Think about it for a minute. What if they are a smoke-screen?"

Her hazel eyes narrowed. "You think Bitsy's boy-friend wrote them?"

"Right. And that means he knows a lot about Friars' Academy. He would have to be on the faculty."

She looked at me quizzically. "Ann, I can't picture it. Not Pat or Steve . . . or Clay."

"Somebody killed Oscar," I said irritably.

But she did find their folders for me.

Pat Porter was a little older than I'd thought. He was nudging thirty. He was from Long Beach and he had earned his BFA at UCLA. He had a long string of acting credits and letters of recommendation from two drama coaches.

Dodie flicked a stubby finger against the bio sheet. "He's single, Ann. So what would keep him from marrying Bitsy if he were the daddy-to-be?"

"He's engaged to Carlos Contreras' daughter."

"Oh-h-h-h."

"And he's trying for a part in Contreras' new picture. How long do you think he would last if Consuelo booted him?"

We read Steve Tibbets' folder next. When we had finished, Dodie said wryly, "If Steve has any guilty secrets, they aren't listed."

Then we came to Clay.

We were a little constrained.

"Look, Ann, I can see why you might think it would be Clay. I can see why Bitsy would fall in love with him."

She understood that. She had been there herself and she was a lot older and wiser than Bitsy.

"But, Ann, for God's sake. Clay isn't a monster. I don't think he would dump Bitsy if she got pregnant. In fact . . ." and her broad plain face flushed a little, "I think he would have dumped June and married Bitsy. He told me once how much he wished he had children."

"Good grief, Dodie, can you imagine the scandal? Why, Clay would have lost his job and never gotten another one at any school in California!"

Dodie shrugged. "He should care."

"Well, I guess it's easy to see the other guy's career go kaput but it's tough to get teaching jobs anymore. And, frankly, what else could Clay do? I mean, good looks are great but they don't bring in a lot of money."

"Clay doesn't have to teach or do any damn thing he doesn't want to." Dodie gave a short little laugh. "He's a gentleman teacher if there ever was one. Hell, Ann, the Fredericks are rich. Like your family."

I started to answer that. My family isn't rich at all. Dad is a surgeon and a good one and he makes a bundle of money but I had known enough truly rich kids at Friars' Academy to understand the distinction between the upper middle class and the upper class. But money, like looks, is in the eye of the beholder. To Dodie, struggling to make car and tuition payments, we were rich. I let it go.

"You don't think it's Clay," and I suppose I said it too gently.

Her face reddened again. "I just don't think he would have had a real motive even if he were the man," she said stiffly.

Well, after all, she had been to bed with him and I hadn't. And it was hard to picture easygoing, delightful Clay planning a murder. If he could sit on a vine-shaded lanai and push a button to banish a threat, maybe so. But to stand behind a boy he knew and shove a thin, sharp instrument into his back?

Still, I reached over and picked up Clay's folder. He was from Gulfport, Mississippi. That explained the soft lazy lilt to his voice. Everybody knew there were a lot of rich southerners.

My eyes skipped down the lines. Clay had attended a teacher's college in Biloxi.

That didn't sound like money.

After a couple of years in the Army, he came to California and earned an MA from Berkeley. He was a graduate assistant there then taught at a private school in San Francisco. In 1965, he'd married June Hasley in Stockton. The next year he joined the faculty at Friars' Academy.

"Where did Clay get his money?"

Dodie shrugged. "He inherited it, I guess."

"Didn't he go to a teacher's college?"

"Yeah."

"Rich southerners go to WA and Vanderbilt and Sewanee."

"Maybe he had lousy grades. For heaven's sake, Ann,

what possible difference could it make where Clay went to college?"

"If he was a poor boy who went to a teacher's college then made it through Berkeley on the GI Bill, he isn't rich."

"Ann, I've been to their house. You can't see the roof! And it has a greenhouse and a swimming-pool and a cabana and a putting-green. You name it, they've got it."

"Right, and that takes a lot of money. But look at it, Dodie, what if the money belongs to June?"

TEN

I had to hurry like hell if I was going to meet Bill at the Racquet Club. I was running late since I'd stayed so long at school, talking to Dodie and studying the files. I was tempted when I got home to call Bill and make an excuse. Or, frankly, to tell him I was mixed up in a murder investigation and hot on the trail. My hand was on the receiver when I remembered something else. This would be the third Saturday Bill and I had played at the Club and each time before we had seen the Fredericks. We had always smiled and nodded hello, the way you do when you see acquaintances.

But maybe I could improve on that.

I was relieved not to see Bill's MG when I careened into the Club parking lot. I jumped out of the Rabbit and hurried up the broad wooden steps of the clubhouse. The reservation desk was just inside the main door.

Pete, who played tennis at USC and was beautiful, blond and tanned a golden brown, sat behind the desk. He looked tired. Saturdays at a tennis club aren't restful for the help.

I looked back over my shoulder. No sign yet of Bill. I waited impatiently while Pete dealt with two phone calls, sold a can of balls and took a racket to be restrung. When it was my turn, I gave another swift glance over my shoulder.

"Fleeing from the Mounties?" Pete asked.

"Shut up," I replied pleasantly. "Look, Pete, I want you to do me a favour."

"Honey, if you don't have a reservation, I couldn't get you on if your last name were Brown."

"Oh, we've got one. But I want to know which court. Abshier and Farrell."

"Court 9."

"Okay. Where are the Fredericks playing?"

He looked at me curiously then obediently checked the reservation sheet.

"Fourteen."

"Can you switch us with the people on 13?"

He thought a minute. "Sure. They aren't here yet and they'll never know the difference. But your date may."

"How's that?"

Pete grinned. "He asked for 9 especially. It's one of two we call lovers' courts. Man, they are screened by pines. All the way around." He leered.

"Did your mother ever tell you it wasn't polite to make faces?"

"No, but she warned me to be on the look-out for beautiful dark-haired girls because they might be hazardous to my health." Then, looking behind me, his face reformed into polite attention. "Hello, Mr. Abshier. You and Miss Farrell are on Court 13."

"But I thought . . ." Bill began.

I swung around and took his arm. "Let's get some tea to take down with us, Bill."

Bill had stopped. "I thought we were going to be on 9."

"Oh, it's some mix-up in the reservations. I told Pete we'd be glad to take 13."

"Oh. Well. All right, Ann. If you don't mind."

"Not at all." I smiled up at him. Then his eyes looked me over and he began to smile, too. I was glad I had worn my new tennis dress.

The Fredericks were already playing when we came onto Court 13. We settled our things on the bench alongside then began to warm up. When Clay and June changed sides, I waved my racket at them.

"Hi, June. Hi, Clay. Beautiful day, isn't it?"

"Oh hello, Ann. Hi, Bill. Good to see you," and Clay smiled his charming, easy smile. June nodded pleasantly.

Was it a guilty conscience or had she looked at me very intently?

We played two sets and Bill had a really good time. He beat me 6-3, 6-4. Frankly, I can beat him but I was having a little trouble with my concentration. I was so aware of Clay and June. They were, for their ages, in super shape. Clay, of course, was fortyish and June, I supposed, a little younger. He was a good solid player but she made him work for every point. Her timing was excellent. She played a baseline game, long hard shots that bounced high and fast, pinning him back. She used her height and strength to advantage. She was almost as tall as Clay and strongly built. They played with no emotion, a few quiet calls of "Good shot."

Towards the end of our third set, I made a desperate sideways lunge for Bill's passing shot, barely got it, then began to backpedal, expecting his put-away, and put on a frantic burst of speed when he lofted a high deep lob. It bounced on the baseline as I was pursuing it and I skidded to a stop on the dusty grey clay, my hair dangling in damp tendrils, sweat pouring down my face, panting. I happened to glance at the other court. June was returning a forehand with a powerful down the line shot. It was just out of Clay's reach.

It was hard to believe, looking at Clay, that he could possibly be involved in anything as ugly as murder. He saw me looking at him and flashed his graceful, good-humoured smile.

The next players for Court 13 were waiting as Bill and I played our last game. I was watching the Fredericks out of the corner of my eye. They started to gather up their rackets. I double-faulted at thirty-all, then hit a back-hand into the net at thirty-forty. I ran lightly toward the net to grin at Bill.

"Hey, that was fun. Ready for something to drink?"

"Sure."

We turned toward the bench to gather up our racket covers and I called out to Clay and June.

"Won't you join us on the verandah for a drink?"

"Sure," Clay replied immediately. Then he glanced at June. "Okay?"

She nodded graciously and slipped her peach warm-up jacket over her shoulders, leaving Clay to carry both rackets. I noticed they were Yonexes and her warm-up was by a name designer and sold for around two hundred dollars.

I picked up my own racket and fell into step beside June. I could sense Bill's surprise as he followed with Clay but he wasn't angry. He was so darn nice. I felt a little pang that I didn't like him more.

I steered everyone toward a corner of the verandah and a clump of white wicker chairs encircling a wicker table. While Bill and Clay were gone to get the drinks, I tried to think how to find out if June was born to money. How to start? Well, the trick to any interview is to get your subject talking. I was still fishing in my mind for a beginning when June said quietly, "It must have been very upsetting for you."

I looked at her blankly. In turn she looked a little flustered. "You were the one who found Oscar's body, weren't you? Oh, maybe you don't want to talk about it. I didn't intend . . ."

"Oh no, no," I interrupted. "I don't mind. I mean, it was awful, looking down into the ravine and seeing him there."

"How did you happen . . . ?" She trailed off, perhaps wondering how tactful her question might be. I swept right into my story. I'd told it so often now that it had a lack of reality to me. A set piece.

She shook her head and her violet eyes were huge and luminous. "Oh, that's terrible, just terrible. But he died much earlier, didn't he?"

I nodded. "He was last seen at two o'clock and he was killed before the rain started at 3:14."

June shivered. "Oh, that's awful. I was on the campus then."

"You were?"

She nodded solemnly. "I dropped by Clay's office, oh, I'm not exactly sure of the time, but I knew it was just before it rained because we were held up by the rain. I came by to see if he wanted to go to the new exhibit at the County Art Museum."

Clay offices in Callison Hall, the long, low slung building separated from the *Herald* office by the thick stand of pines.

"Oh," I said slowly, "did you find him?"

She looked surprised. "Oh yes, he doesn't have any classes after two."

"What did you do?"

She looked at me strangely.

I rushed ahead. "I was thinking, if you and Clay came out after the rain and took the path by the pine trees, you might have noticed someone walking toward the *Herald* Building." It would have been just about the time I had heard the outer door open and someone had gone into the news-room and, I felt sure, taken the paper from Oscar's typewriter and left the pink pad and list in his desk.

June was frowning in recollection. "I left before Clay. He had some more papers to grade and we were in separate cars.

I did go that way, but I didn't see a soul."

I wanted very much to ask her if Clay had been his usual urbane self when she arrived, but there wasn't any way to do that. And, certainly, her arrival alibied him for part of the critical time.

"Did you tell the police lieutenant about this?"

She nodded. Then she looked past me and waved to some friends. No wonder she was so relaxed. Clay had her word that he was in his office during part of the time when Oscar was meeting his killer. I wondered briefly if June knew about the pink slips? I studied her calm untroubled face. Would she care?

Would she lie for Clay?

Then I felt a spark of shame. How determined was I to tie the murder to Clay? For heaven's sake, everything I learned worked to clear him. He didn't have to worry about holding a job. His marriage was apparently a success no matter what his proclivities. Why didn't I drop it, let the lieutenant do his job?

And let him arrest Dodie Wingate?

Clay and Bill were laughing as they came back to the table, carrying gin and tonics. As they sat down, Bill was saying, "Of course, not just any energy stock is the answer." Clay was nodding sagely.

I turned back to June. "What do you think about the murder?"

She shrugged. "Who knows? Anyway, it was probably suicide. You know how teenagers are. Up and down. That's the answer."

I shook my head. "Oh no, June. It couldn't have been suicide. Someone stabbed him in the back."

"Well," she said stubbornly, "Maybe he twisted his arm back there and did it. He was a weird kid."

"Not that weird," I said shortly.

"Oh, I forgot," she said apologetically. "I know you liked him, but it seems to me that it was an odd thing to happen. Especially at a place like Friars' Academy. If it wasn't suicide, then it must have been a nut."

"A nut?"

"You know," she responded. "Some beatnik or religious freak. There are thousands of them around."

Yes, there were thousands in Southern California but the Friars' Academy campus didn't exactly teem with them.

"Are you from California?" I asked.

She looked a little surprised and I didn't blame her but I had to find out more about her and soon. Bill was not going to be content to spend the rest of the afternoon with the Fredericks.

"Yes. Stockton."

"Did you grow up there?"

She nodded. "It's a nice city."

"I'm sure it is. Really, Northern California is nicer."

We balanced the relative merits of Stockton and La Villita and I would have been bored out of my mind if I hadn't been tenaciously pursuing an objective.

June gave me an easy opening.

"Of course," she said sagely, "it's always nice to live in a university town. It offers so many cultural advantages."

"Did you attend the University of the Pacific?"

She nodded.

"Is that where you and Clay met?" and I smiled fatuously.

"Oh no, I was out of school and teaching when we met."

"But I suppose you were married in Stockton?"

"Yes."

"In June? I love June weddings."

She smiled. "Oh yes, I was a June bride."

Bill was looking from one of us to the other, trying to

102

follow our conversation and I pitied him. I beamed a smile at him.

"Bill, we're going to have to say goodbye to these nice people. I promised Mother we would drop by after we had played tennis."

His smile turned a little fixed and I didn't blame him. When we were out in the lot, I gave a sigh of relief. "I don't know what possessed me to ask them to join us," I said untruthfully.

"Oh, that's all right," Bill replied. "He's going to drop by the office Monday and let me take a look at his portfolio, so it wasn't a waste."

"Good. By the way, we don't have to go by my folks but I thought you might want to go for a dip."

It made Mother's afternoon. We swam in the heated pool for an hour then fixed hamburgers on the charcoal grill. We had fun and I still managed to say good-night to Bill and get back to McDonough Hall by seven.

I was hoping for a phone call. And I had several calls to make.

The first was a person-to-person call to Celia Anders who was assistant lay-out editor of the Stockton morning paper.

"Cee, this is Ann Farrell . . . yes . . . it has been a long time . . . well, I never get up that way. Listen, Cee, will you do me a favour and check your files, I need some info for an investigative story. It shouldn't take you long. I want the name of the bride's parents from a wedding story that would have been published in June 1965. The groom's name was Clay Fredericks and the bride's, June Halsey."

It might take a while but I was going to find out more about Clay and June. If the money belonged to her, well, that would be motive enough for Clay to go to great lengths to keep her in the dark about any off-the-reservation frolics.

Clay liked money. I was sure of that. Sex, too, but I would bet he loved money more.

I glanced at the clock. Seven-thirty. Dodie had said Seth would leave by seven for his monthly poker game and I could call her then to see what she had been able to find out about Steve Tibbets and Pat Porter.

She answered on the first ring.

"Did you talk to Steve?" I asked.

"Yes. I dropped by his apartment. He lives in the Sand Castle complex just off Crewes Drive. And, Ann, if it's Steve Tibbets, I'll eat his track shoes."

"Why do you say that?"

"To begin with, this voluptuous black-haired gal answered the door and Steve just introduced her as Judy, his friend. Well, you know what that means these days. Anyway, I gave them this lame story that I was out rustling up donations from faculty members to buy a wreath for Oscar's funeral. It's Monday, by the way, and school will be dismissed. Steve said, sure, so I took a couple of bucks and hung in the doorway and said, well, it sure had been a sad year for the Academy and he looked kind of surprised and said, oh, yeah, and I said, you know, this coming right on the heels of the tragedy about Bitsy. And, Ann, I swear to God he had no idea what I was talking about. It was Judy who spoke up and said sure, didn't he remember, that was the Friars' Academy girl who had drowned, oh, just after Christmas. He still looked blank, then Judy said, Oh, well, of course, he didn't remember because he had gone home to New Jersey to visit his folks and was out of town when it happened."

It sounded reasonable enough. I hadn't pinned a lot of hope on Steve Tibbets anyway.

"How about Pat Porter?"

"Well," she said slowly, "if there's anything to your

104

theory, he might be the one because something certainly does have him spooked."

His apartment wasn't far from Steve's so she had decided to give it a try, once again with her plea for funds for a faculty donated wreath.

Pat had stepped out into the hall, closing his apartment door behind him, his handsome face sullen and uncooperative.

"Yeah, well, look, Mrs. Wingate, I didn't even know the kid."

"He was in your Modern Drama class," Dodie objected.

"Yeah, but I mean I didn't *know* him." Pat jammed a hand into his pocket, "And I don't have any money right now."

By this time, Dodie was wondering why he was so intent on keeping her out of his apartment.

"A cheque would be fine," she replied blandly.

But he stood stubbornly in the hall, his head turned a little as if trying to hear through the closed door to his apartment. When the door jerked open, alarm flared in his eyes.

The girl who peered around him at Dodie was short and heavy with a pudgy dark face and small pudgy hands that reached up to cling possessively to Pat's arm. "Who's your friend, Pat?"

"Connie, this is Mrs. Wingate, a counsellor at Friars' Academy. Mrs. Wingate, this is Consuelo Contreras, my fiancée."

The quick suspicious look in Connie's eyes died.

"Mrs. Wingate's collecting money for some flowers for that kid's funeral. You know, the one that got killed."

"Oh." Connie was satisfied now. "How much do you want?"

"Oh, whatever, a dollar or two from every faculty member will . . ."

Connie was already turning to go back inside. In a moment, she clumped heavily back to the door, a five-dollar bill in her hand. She thrust it out.

Dodie began to thank her but Connie was ignoring her, looking up at Pat, tugging on his arm, her pudgy face absorbed, adoring.

Pat flung a "See you, Mrs. Wingate" over his shoulder. After the door had closed, Dodie stood there for a long moment. Pat, she thought, was going to pay dearly for that role in the next Contreras movie.

"So Pat's pretty uptight?"

"I'll say," Dodie responded. "I can believe he wouldn't want Connie to know if he'd been messing around with somebody else. Especially someone as pretty as Bitsy. That Contreras woman is about as sexy as an eggplant. He couldn't possibly be in love with her."

"No, I don't imagine he is."

"And how did you get on?" she asked.

"Oh, I played some tennis with Bill Abshier and we had a drink with Clay and June. I'll have to admit, Dodie, that Clay's awfully cool and relaxed. You would think he doesn't have a care in the world."

"I don't think he does," she said dryly.

"Maybe not. Anyway, I'm still trying to find out who has the chips."

We said goodnight and I got up and roamed around the room. Pat or Clay? Clay or Pat? Or, as Dodie would insist, someone else unknown?

The phone rang.

I jumped for it and was surprised at myself.

But it was Cee.

"Oh great, you got it? . . . Mr. and Mrs. Alvin James Hasley of 413 Mission . . . great, Cee. Are they socially prominent? . . . Hmm . . . Listen, Cee, I really appreciate your help."

I studied the address which I had underlined with three dark lines. 413 Mission. It was an older part of Stockton which Cee didn't know very well. And she didn't know the name Hasley. It hadn't figured in the Stockton social notes since Cee had been there. She had checked the current directory and Alvin J. Hasley was still listed at that address and Cee had given me the telephone number.

Did the money belong to Clay or June? I still didn't know, but I was going to find out. If the money belonged to Clay, then my carefully thought out motive wasn't there.

I leaned back in my chair. Damn, it still seemed impossible to visualize Clay slamming a knife into Oscar's back. Maybe I was off on a wild-goose chase. Maybe Oscar had written those pink notes and one of the recipients had gone for him.

After all, and it was a small wormy thought wriggling in the recesses of my mind, Oscar did have a peculiar sense of humour. He had carried a worn and tattered copy of Ambrose Bierce. He might have thought it really a rag to compose those notes and watch the responses. I stared down at the sheet of paper. Well, I wouldn't give up just yet. I was reaching for my pencil when the phone rang again.

This time it was the call I'd been hoping for.

ELEVEN

He must have been at the nearest pay-phone because it didn't take him quite five minutes to arrive. I was watching from my dormer window and I hurried down to answer the door.

For an instant, I had trouble breathing. I had never felt quite this way before. Not even for Michael. I had never before had such a vivid awareness of a man's nearness, of the way his polo shirt stretched across his chest, of the way he stood, of the space between us.

He stepped toward me. "Ann," he began. Then he stopped, clenched his hands, "Miss Farrell."

"Ann," I said quickly, "My name is Ann," but the mood was broken.

He grinned again, a little wryly. "A police detective isn't supposed to become friends with . . . with the subjects in an investigation."

"My name is Ann," I said stubbornly. "What's yours?"

He laughed then, "Alonzo."

"Alonzo," I repeated. It suited him. It was as different as he was.

"Alonzo Fox, Cherokee Indian from Tahlequah, Oklahoma."

He had come a long way to be here, a long way in time and space and we both knew it. Standing in an old wooden Victorian house in the California hills, a girl from a melange of Scotch, Irish, English and Spanish background and a Cherokee Indian from Oklahoma. However diverse our heritage, there was a bond between us. We both knew that, too.

We went up to my suite and I fixed us a drink and when we were settled on the short rather lumpy sofa in front of the fireplace, another Victorian plus, I looked at him curiously. "So you're an Okie?"

"Not really," he said quickly. "Okies are the poor whites who straggled out to California during the Dust Bowl days in rattletrap cars with mattresses tied on top." He laughed shortly. "Poor Indians never had any land to lose and sure never had any kind of car, even rattletraps, to drive." He stared at the flames for a moment, then shrugged. "Though I guess I could qualify as a latter-day Okie. I used the GI Bill to finance my relocation."

"Why California?"

"Why not? It's the dreamland of America, isn't it? Even a poor Indian kid could see a rainbow out here." He paused. "Oh hell, Ann, it's a long boring story. You wouldn't be interested."

"I would."

He looked at me steadily for a moment, then slowly smiled. "The Growing Up of Alonzo Fox?"

And in his low husky voice he evoked for me a picture of a life I had never known, long easy summer days with heat thick and palpable as soft tar, grimmer winter days huddling around a wood fire in a one-room shanty. A woman-dominated world of his grandmother, mother and sister.

". . . never knew my dad. He was killed in an oil-rig accident when I was about two."

But it had been a happy childhood. "Mom worked at a laundry in town. She ironed shirts. All day she stood there, winter, summer, lifting the press, pushing it down." Never enough money but lots of laughter and fry bread when times were hard, miles of country to explore, twisty half-dry creek beds and gnarled black jack groves. And, after high school, he joined the Marines.

His mother died during his second tour in Viet Nam. When that stint ended, he decided not to re-enlist and he stayed in California.

"I worked as a police dispatcher and went to college. I'd decided to be a cop." He paused then said crisply. "That's my story, Ann. What's yours?"

I told him. When I finished, I looked around the narrow room, "This is just a way-station. I don't know where I'll go from here."

"Who does?" he said quietly. Then he smiled. "But I'm glad you're here and I'm glad I've met you. Both because I like you and because I think you're the person who can help me now. You will, won't you?"

His question was simple and direct and I knew what he was asking. Ours is a funny culture. You learn early on that it isn't attractive to snitch on your fellows.

He watched me, his dark eyes grave. He knew what I was thinking.

"Killers are dangerous, Ann."

I knew that. And I wanted to trap Oscar's killer. Not just to safeguard society. Not for such a noble purpose. My feeling was more basic. I didn't want the bastard to get away with it. Oscar had been alive and now he was dead and that shouldn't be.

"Yes. I'll help."

"I talked to Mrs. Wingate. I talked to her at school as you asked me to." He shook his head irritably. "Hell, I'm trying to give her a break. But she just won't ante. Ann, I've got to know. Why is she on that list?"

I stared down at the fire.

"I'm going to talk to her husband in the morning."

"Alonzo, no!"

He shoved a hand through his straight black hair. "I don't have any choice. She won't talk and she has no alibi. And she's scared to death. I'm sure of that. I can smell it."

"Sure, she's scared. She's scared out of her mind that Seth is going to find out."

"Find out what?"

"That she had an affair with Clay Fredericks."

"Oh," Alonzo said slowly. "Oh, yeah. I see it now. Fredericks admitted getting a pink slip but he wouldn't say what it was about. He smiled and said he had to protect the lady's name."

Oh yes, of course. Clay would enjoy being a gentleman. I could hear it all now. But he really wouldn't care. It was Dodie who cared.

"Dodie'd rather die than have Seth find out," and I told Alonzo how I had found her, sitting in her darkened office at school that afternoon.

"So she'd rather die. Maybe she would rather kill than have him know?"

I remembered Dodie's flushed face at the *Herald* office on Friday. She was going to shake Belinda Bascomb until her neck cracked. "Look, Alonzo, Dodie talked to me Friday morning about the pink notes. It was while she was waiting to be interviewed. I swear to God she thought Belinda Bascomb had written them. She was just out of her mind with fury and she was going to break Belinda's neck."

"Out of her mind with fury," he repeated softly.

"But don't you seee? If she thought Belinda wrote the notes then she wouldn't have had any reason to kill Oscar. She didn't have a motive."

"If she killed Oscar, she'd be pretty sure to make it clear to someone that she didn't think Oscar had written the notes."

So that's what Alonzo thought, that I was a chump set up by Dodie to bolster her story.

"She has a motive, the opportunity, and she's big and strong enough to have handled Oscar's body. I'll tell you, Ann, she looks good to me."

"But she isn't the only one on that list. What about the others?"

"I'm working on them. You don't need to worry about that. I'm interested in Casteel, but I don't rank his motive as high. He might get fired but he didn't seem too worried about it."

"What's his secret?"

"He's a bookie."

"Oh. Oh, I see." So that was how Paul financed those trips to Africa and his taste for native sculpture.

"And Jennifer?"

Alonzo smiled. "Mrs. Prince is quite a woman. She looked straight at me with absolutely no change of expression and insisted she didn't have any idea what I was talking about. 'What notes?' she asked. But she has a talkative neighbour, a Mrs. Kelly, who couldn't wait to tell me all about the young men who come to Mrs. Prince's apartment. 'Not even half her age!' "

I nodded. I'd thought it would be something of that kind. But, unless Jennifer got involved in some sort of public scandal, the school wouldn't have any reason to ever know or care what she did at home.

"Right now, Belinda Bascomb and Dodie Wingate look like the best bets," Alonzo said.

"What about Pat Porter? And Clay?"

Alonzo leaned back and frowned thoughtfully. "So far, we haven't come up with anything on Porter. I'm sure there's something there because he was so damn nervous he couldn't sit still when we talked to him. But he had a three o'clock play practice. He was a little late but he would have had to rush like hell to get to the *Herald* office and back in the break after his two o'clock class. He would have had only twelve to fifteen minutes at the most. Is that long enough to meet Oscar, quarrel, kill him and throw him over the balcony?"

"And Clay?" I persisted.

"Oh, I can't see Fredericks as a killer. He admits to getting a pink slip but very cheerfully. He grinned at me and said he wasn't at liberty to name the woman but he was very unruffled about the whole thing. And he said he just dismissed it from his mind and had no idea who had written it. He looked quite surprised when I said it was Oscar. Besides, his wife found him in his office between two and three. I think we can let him out."

"It's just a partial alibi."

Alonzo shrugged. "That's the kind that rings true. They aren't sure of the time. She just dropped in then stayed until the rain was over. She left before him because they were in two cars. Very casual. I think you can wash out Fredericks, Ann."

I didn't answer.

"Ann?"

"Yes."

"Are you still off on this idea that whoever got Bitsy Martin pregnant murdered Oscar?"

"Yes."

He gave a little sigh of exasperation. "Ann, that's just too complicated. Murder is simple. We know Oscar was threatening these people, threatening their jobs, their marriages, their reputations . . ."

"But we don't know that!" I insisted. "Just because you

found that wad of pink notes in Oscar's pocket doesn't mean he wrote them."

"His fingerprints are on the pad that was found in his pocket."

"So the murderer put Oscar's hands on the pad. How about that other pad, the one I found in his desk?"

"All right. It doesn't have Oscar's prints. But maybe he wore gloves when he filched that one."

"How about the note to me? Does it have his prints on it?"

"No, but again he was probably careful with the ones he sent out."

"But he just stuffed that pad into his pocket willy-nilly?"

"He was under a strain so he might have done anything."

"He was under a strain because of Bitsy!"

"Look, Ann, the list you found in his desk did have his fingerprints on it."

"That's easy. Somebody typed it at his desk and used paper from his drawer. The paper could easily have his fingerprints on it. And the murderer wore gloves."

"That's possible," Alonzo said equably, "but consider this. If Oscar didn't write those notes then someone else wrote them and either Oscar discovered the writer's identity and was killed or the notes were written purposefully to make Oscar look like their author and to provide a reason for his murder."

"Yes, yes, yes."

"But that would mean that Oscar's murder had been planned ahead because Belinda Bascomb received her note more than a week before he was killed."

"Right."

"So you think Oscar was threatening to make trouble for Bitsy Martin's boy-friend and he planned this complicated method of murder?"

"Not so complicated," I objected. "If the man is a faculty member, or to put it plainly, if he is Pat or Clay, all he has to do is get a fresh pad of slips from a supply closet, keeping his fingerprints off of it, write the notes, and anybody on the faculty could know enough to write them, deliver them, give time for the notes to get people aroused, then make an appointment with Oscar at the *Herald* office, meet him, stab him, take a pad and put Oscar's prints on it, stuff it in his pocket and throw him off the balcony. Then, later, he must have remembered that sheet in Oscar's typewriter and decided not to take a chance on leaving it there. When he came to get it, he put more pink pads in the drawer and typed up that nice little list just to help the police along. What's so complicated about that?"

"What if someone had seen this person leaving a poison-pen note."

"As important as it was not to be seen, don't you imagine he was very, very careful?"

Alonzo wasn't convinced, but he did listen to my final plea.

"I know you aren't persuaded but find out two things, Alonzo. Find out what Pat Porter's hiding and find out where the Fredericks' money comes from."

"What do the Frederick's finances have to do with anything?"

I told him my theory then. I didn't think Clay would go to the lengths of murder to keep June because of love. But he might do it for money. "What if the money belongs to June?"

"I'll find out if I can. But, Ann, she doesn't look to me like the type to kick him out because he was slipping around. I'd say they both probably have other . . . friends."

I was afraid he was right, but I still clung to my idea. If June had the money.

When Alonzo got up to go, I walked to the door with him and we stood there for a long moment.

He didn't kiss me. He almost did. I knew that. And I knew that one night soon he would.

I was in bed, but not sleepy, lying there watching a thin strand of moonlight move across the wall, when the phone rang. I rolled over and grabbed up the receiver.

"Hello."

"Miss Farrell?"

"Yes?"

"This is Shannon Kirk."

Excitement flared. "Yes, Shannon. What is it?"

"Miss Farrell, I've been thinking it over and I thought I should call you."

I was sitting up now, gripping the receiver so tightly. Was I going to know? Clay or Pat? Pat or Clay?

"I don't really know anything definite but I can tell you one thing."

"Yes, Shannon, what is it?"

"I don't know who the man was. She never would tell me. She just said he was so handsome and . . . and wonderful and she loved him so much."

My shoulders slumped. Oh hell, she didn't know.

"She wouldn't tell me his name but I know where she used to meet him."

TWELVE

It was a dusty down-at-heel apartment complex. There are thousands of them off the main drags, pink and yellow and faded blue stucco with interior squares of grass and one or two palms. This one sported a Moorish arch and a sidewalk that had been painted red. I looked around the courtyard. It was eerily quiet, a somnolent Sunday morning quiet. Newspapers lay ungathered in front of four apartments.

"Are you looking for an apartment?"

I jumped a little then turned to face the speaker. She was about my age but so skinny her levis just hung on her hips and her worn black Doobie Bros. T-Shirt looked enormous. She had scraggly blond hair and bad teeth and a nervous, harried look. The baby she carried on one hip looked too heavy for her to handle.

"We got a vacancy in Number 3."

"I'm not looking for an apartment. I just wanted to talk to you for a moment."

She took a step back, her eyes wary. "Yeah?"

"Wait, please. Let me explain. It's about my sister."

"Your sister?"

"I'm hunting for her and someone I know said they'd seen her here." I was fumbling in my purse for the picture of Bitsy that I had cut out of the yearbook.

The girl took the picture. She looked at it for a long moment then raised her eyes to mine and I knew she had recognized it.

"You've seen her?"

"Look, lady, I don't run an answering service or nothin'."

"Please, we've been hunting for her for more than a month."

She jiggled the baby on her hip. "A runaway, huh?"

"Yes, and my folks are just crazy."

She held the picture up to the light, giving herself a little more time. Oh damn, I was so close!

"I just want to talk to her. There won't be any trouble, I promise you that."

She looked at me dubiously.

"She's just sixteen and I know if I can talk to her . . ."

"You aren't gonna call the cops or anything . . . ?"

"No. No, I just want a chance to talk to her."

The baby began to cry and the girl humped him up over her shoulder. "Well, I don't suppose it will do any harm to tell you what I know. Sure, lady, I've seen her but you're too late to catch her. It's been three, four weeks since she's been here."

Yes, Bitsy Martin had lain in her grave almost three weeks now.

"She used to come at the week-ends to Apt. 7." She nodded to her right. "Mr. Baker's apartment. But it's been a long time since she's come. Mr. Baker is usually only here at week-ends himself. He's a travelling salesman, works for some encyclopedia company and he's on the road weekdays."

So he came at weekends. I was pulling another picture out of my handbag. This one was larger than Bitsy's. Faculty members are permitted three by five's instead of two by three's. I held it out to her.

"Oh, that's him," she agreed readily then she looked at me

suspiciously. "How come you have his picture, too? Hey, lady, what's going on?"

"Nothing. I just . . . wanted to be sure who . . . she was with."

She looked suddenly sympathetic. "Hey, lady, I'm sorry."

"Oh, it's not . . ."

But she had already made up her mind. She was smiling a little crookedly at me. "Lady, it doesn't do any good to know."

I felt very sad. Not for the reason she assumed, but for another. I liked Clay. It was impossible not to like Clay, unruffled, pleasant, good-humoured Clay. And this cheap apartment house with its straggling patch of grass and rusted lawn furniture made him seem tawdry. Hadn't it almost made Bitsy cry to come here? How could this have been exciting, a haven for lovers? When she headed her sailboat out that last morning was this sleazy cheaply stuccoed building what she remembered?

The girl put up a thin hand to touch my arm. "Go on home, lady. Give it up."

I shook my head. "No. Not yet. I'm going to see if he is here." I turned and walked across the grass toward Number 7. I could feel her watching me.

What was I going to do if Clay opened the door? What could I say?

The sun-faded white curtains at the single front window hung straight and closed. The knock echoed a little but there was not a sound from beyond the yellow door.

I rattled the knob.

It was hard to couple Clay, elegant immaculate Clay, with that apartment. I turned and walked slowly away, sad and puzzled and half wishing I'd never come. Maybe Alonzo was right and Bitsy and her lover had nothing to do with Oscar's death. Then who was I to come along, raking up yesterday's indiscretion? Clay wasn't a monster and, if he had loved Bitsy, he must have grieved at her death. So why didn't I leave ill enough alone? It could only cause trouble for Clay and June and the Martins if I kept after it.

But there was a core of stubbornness in me. I didn't think Oscar had written those notes and I did think his death was connected with Bitsy's and now I knew that Clay was the man who had driven Bitsy to suicide.

What would Clay do to hide that fact?

He didn't have to worry about a job. He was rich. Obviously he taught as an avocation. Rich, secure, caught up in a world of tennis and sailing and travel, he might not like a scandal but it couldn't hurt him. He and June had the good life. They cruised to South America every summer, often taking a Friars' Academy student or two along as crew. In fact, Oscar had gone with them once or twice.

Would Clay kill someone he knew that well, no matter what the cause? And what could Oscar do, after all? There was no question of accusing Clay of being more than the moral cause of Bitsy's death. She had committed suicide. Her sister knew it, had received a note from her that could prove it. The most Oscar could do would be to cause Clay to lose a job he didn't need.

And his wife?

I drove absently, poking along in the slow right lane of the freeway. Would June be angry enough over Bitsy to leave Clay?

I didn't know.

How can anyone make that kind of judgment about someone else's marriage? June had been married to Clay for a long time.

If she didn't know he wandered, she must be very obtuse

or he must be very careful. If she did know, then what difference would one more make? If she didn't know, then the possibility existed that she might not tolerate unfaithfulness.

But, for God's sake, Bitsy was dead! She certainly was no threat now. Would June dump Clay for something in the past?

Only if she were very imperious and rigid.

Even if she left him, would Clay care all that much?

Only if the money belonged to her. If the scandal could cost Clay his cushy life, he might turn very dangerous indeed.

Back at McDonough Hall, I fixed myself an avocado and cheese on rye and drank white wine and watched the clock. I judged one-thirty would be about the right time to catch either churchgoers or Sunday-morning sleepers at home.

I used direct long distance dialling. As I dialled, I looked at my notes from last night. Mr. and Mrs. Alvin James Hasley announce the marriage of their daughter, June Clair, to Mr. Clay Andrew Fredericks at seven P.M. on Saturday, June 12, 1965, in the Lewiston Chapel of Grace Methodist Church.

"Hello." Her voice sounded faded and quavery.

"Mrs. Hasley? Mrs. Alvin James Hasley?"

"Oh yes, yes," and there was a note of alarm in her voice.

"Mrs. Hasley, this is Consumer Research Service calling from Los Angeles. Would you have a moment today to help us with a telephone survey? We have nothing to sell but are solely seeking information for an advertising union. If you do agree to talk to us, we will put a small gift of cologne in the mail to you today and the gift, of course, will be free of charge."

"Oh. Well, I guess so. What do you want to ask?"

"We have a series of questions, Mrs. Hasley, that will help us determine where to offer our product, which must remain nameless to protect our research."

"Oh, I understand."

Which was more than I did.

"Thank you so much, Mrs. Hasley. Now, can you tell me how long you have lived at your present address?"

"Poppa and I bought our house here in 1936. It was a brand new section of town then. Why, the streetcar didn't even reach out here and now they talk about buying up all this part of town. Urban blight, they talk about, though my place is as well-kept as anybody's."

"How many bedrooms do you have?"

"Two and a sleeping-porch. That's where the boys slept, growing up."

"Is your kitchen gas or electric?"

"We started off with gas and with an icebox on the back porch. I had that all through the war and after but my daughter and son-in-law modernized the kitchen for me a few years ago. They tried to get me to take one of those new-fangled microwave ovens but I told June I was too old to have to learn how to cook all over again."

"How many children do you have?"

"One daughter, June, and the three boys, Alvin Jr., Clyde and Richard."

"What is Mr. Hasley's profession?"

"What's that?"

"What does Mr. Hasley do for a living?"

"Oh, well, Poppa died, it must be five years ago now."

"Oh, I'm sorry, Mrs. Hasley. But what did he do?"

"He was a house-painter."

"Did he have a retirement programme?"

"Oh no, Miss. He was self-employed. Took what jobs he could find but it was never hard to find work. So many new houses, you know, after the war and Alvin was always willing to work. He worked hard all his life."

But he didn't make a bundle of money. Not as a self-employed house-painter. So I knew what I had called to find out.

"Have you ever considered selling your home and moving into a condominium?"

"No. Alvin Jr. lives here in town and his boys keep the place nice for me. No, I don't plan to move anywhere, Miss."

"I want to thank you, Mrs. Hasley, for your help. Our gift of appreciation will be in the mail to you today. Thank you so much."

No money there. I put a big series of heavy black XXX's across Mrs. Hasley's name. June Hasley hadn't come from a rich family and she hadn't earned the money herself, not as a young school teacher. So the money belonged to Clay. I circled Clay's name, around and around.

Maybe it was time to throw out all my ideas and start fresh.

Murder demands an awesome motive.

No one murders unless he sees no other recourse. It was the only way to stop Oscar from . . . from what?

Writing the poison-pen notes?

No.

I hadn't believed it before. I didn't believe it now. The notes were a smoke-screen. The notes. Figure out the notes. Who could have written them?

Only someone who knew a very great deal about Friars' Academy. A faculty member or a student or someone else intimately associated with the campus.

The writer had to know about pink slips. He had to know a great deal of malicious gossip. More, frankly, than I had known. He had to know that the *Herald* office often was empty in the afternoons.

That made a small, quite select, group.

And the writer had to know that I would not be in my second-storey office that afternoon.

Had someone seen me in the Library and seized that instant to . . . to what? Ask Oscar to go there . . . ? No, Oscar was already there. We knew that. He was at the *Herald* office at two o'clock. Katie Bernstein had seen him. He was there and anxiously awaiting me.

But why?

Why would Oscar have thought I would be coming . . . ?

I felt a great swell of emptiness, the same upending sensation you have when a huge wave sweeps you up and up and up and you are flying with the spray and the spume.

Oh God, would I ever learn to follow the rules? I was so disdainful of the trivia which Dr. Howard gloried in that I made it a practice rarely to check my in-box in the faculty mailroom.

I grabbed up a sweater and my keys. Outside, I hesitated then decided it would be quicker to walk.

I ran until I felt a sharp pain in my side. My mind told me to slow down. It was too late to hurry. Days too late to hurry.

I plunged across the foot-bridge, walking so quickly that it was swaying back and forth by the time I reached the other side.

The campus was deserted, of course, the wide gravelled paths empty. I began to run again when I was in sight of the Administrative Building. I unlocked the side entrance, fumbled for an instant with the light switches, then hurried down the hall to the frosted door with the legend MAILROOM in neat black letters. The same key unlocked it. I turned on the light. The old-fashioned oak stand with its rows of letter-boxes loomed directly in front of me.

. . . DAVIS, ELLIOT, EVANS, FARRELL . . .

I snatched down a handful of papers. A flyer advertising ARSENIC AND OLD LACE, a thick folded swath of Xerox paper that reproduced the minutes of the most recent faculty meeting, a coy reminder that the mobile blood bank would be on campus March 29 and all red-blooded faculty members would be expected to prove they weren't turnips (oh, God!), a poetic exhortation against littering and a sheet of yellow copy-paper, folded once, with Ms. Farrell scrawled across the back.

I opened it and read.

Oh, hell! Hell and damnation!

I read it again.

> Dear Ms. Farrell,
> Please be at the *Herald* office at two sharp! I can't ex-plain now but it is very important. I need you to be a witness. Please don't be late. (That could be critical.) I know I can count on you.
>
> Oscar
>
> P.S. Don't tell *anyone*. It will be a big story, too.

Oh hell!

Tears burned at the back of my eyes.

I know I can count on you.

He had. And I hadn't come.

If I had seen the note, I would have come. Oscar knew me well enough to know that. He hadn't even needed to add the tempting bait of a big story. I would have wanted to know what he was up to. Yes. I would have come if I had received that note.

It was Oscar's bad luck that I had taken umbrage at the very first faculty meeting when Dr. Howard had equated the daily check of faculty mailboxes with maturity and responsibility, a kind of red badge of adulthood.

Oh God! I'd said softly to myself. Right up there with the Holy Writ.

It had, of course, been a private and very harmless rebellion. Until last Thursday.

A witness. Oscar wanted me to be a witness. A witness to what?

It sounded almost as if he were on the track of something criminal. Here at Friars' Academy?

I whirled around and snatched up the telephone on the secretary's desk, although it was too late to hurry. I flipped open the directory, found the number and dialled.

"Alonzo? Ann here. Ann Farrell. I've found something more about Oscar. . . ."

THIRTEEN

Alonzo joined me at the funeral Monday morning.

"Have you turned up anything new?" I asked.

"Not much. But we'll keep after it."

Alonzo looked so vividly alive, so dark and ruddy among the pale people swirling by us. He leaned closer to me.

"I think you've been right all along, Ann, at least in part. Oscar didn't write those poison-pen notes. I had Mrs. Jenkins help me and we went through his room thoroughly last night. There's no trace of pink pads, nothing to even hint that he had anything to do with the notes. But we did find a piece of paper stuffed in the pocket of a windbreaker. I've got a Xerox copy of it here."

He pulled an envelope out of his coat pocket, opened it and lifted out the copy.

I recognized Oscar's handwriting. The capitalized words and sprinkling of question marks and dollar signs reminded me immediately of the sheet which had disappeared from his typewriter.

"You remember the sheet I told you about?" I asked excitedly. "The one I saw in Oscar's typewriter Thursday afternoon?"

Alonzo nodded. "Right. It looks like the same kind of stuff and it shows what he had on his mind. It wasn't poison-pen letters."

Alonzo and I had both been on the wrong track, because

these scribblings had nothing to do with Bitsy's death, either. I shivered as I read them.

search/seizure??? N.G., too late state's evidence? Co-conspirator? ck. law? indep. witness? how? demand bigger share???? that's the ticket, have Ms. F. hide, listen Thurs. *HERALD OFFICE* by God, I'm going to get that son of a bitch!!!!

"State's evidence," I said slowly. "Co-conspirator. Do you have any idea at all what's involved?"

"No. But we'll find out," Alonzo said confidently. "Now that we know we are looking for criminal activity, we'll find out." He glanced down at his watch. "I'm going out to school now to check his locker again. We might have missed something in light of this. I'm going to talk to Mrs. Wingate again, too, get a better idea of his friends, the people he hung around with. You might ask around, too, Ann." He smiled down at me. "I'll see you later."

He strode across the bright green grass to his car. I walked more slowly, nodding to people I knew, Dodie, and a clump of other faculty members, including Paul Casteel. Paul was unsmiling. That didn't, of course, mean anything. One does not grin joyously at funerals. But Paul looked grim. And we knew that Paul was involved in illegalities up to his neck. Did he do anything else besides make book? I was hazy, actually, on what bookies did but I had a distinct feeling that one thing led to another. Could he be linked to the Mafia?

Criminal activity. Drugs, of course, came to mind first. But surely Oscar's elaborate plan involved more than the peddling of pills and baggies. Drugs on a large scale?

I saw Pat Porter. He was scurrying a little to catch up with the group around Oscar Charles Howell. Always on the make. What would Pat do to anyone threatening his precious career? Could Pat be the one Oscar was trying to trap? But what could Pat have done, outside the law, that Oscar would know about?

I caught a glimpse of Clay and June, climbing into Clay's dark green Jaguar XL6. I tried to imagine Clay conspiring with Oscar. But whatever for? Clay was rich. Oscar was richer. There has to be a reason why people break the law.

This absorbed me all the way back to the Rabbit. It must have been kicks for Oscar, whatever it was. It couldn't have been for money. Then he had had a change of heart, was that it? Perhaps his grief for Bitsy changed his whole approach to life.

But he was angry, those last few weeks. That didn't sound like a conversion to moral purity.

I wasn't much of a detective. Well, I had done my best. I would leave it now to Alonzo. He was perfectly capable of figuring out what had happened. At least this new development put Dodie in the clear. Oscar's last cryptic notes had specifically said he was going to get that son of a bitch. A man.

I was, in fact, ready to stop worrying over it. In a way, I felt that I had done what I set out to do. Not exactly to clear Oscar's name but to take away the stain of having written the poison-pen letters. I had done that. The rest was up to the police. Now I could pick up the everyday pieces of my life, stop playing detective.

Then, just in front of me, I saw Ian Campbell, and I remembered the day last week, it must have been Monday or Tuesday, when I had seen him deep in conversation with Oscar. They were standing on that squat wooden bridge that humped over Lovers' Lake. Oscar, frowning in concentration, his broad Scandanavian face intent, had loomed over Ian.

"Ian."

He stopped, looked back and smiled. "Hi, Miss Farrell."

I came up beside him. "Ian, did you know Oscar well?"

He shrugged. "Yeah. I guess. At least, I've known him for a long time. Since first grade. But I haven't seen much of Oscar the last few years."

No. The last few years had been busy ones for Ian. He worked on the *Herald* and the annual and carried a full schedule of science courses. He planned to be a marine biologist.

"So you don't know much about what Oscar was doing lately?"

"Not much."

"I saw you talking to him last week. On the bridge over Lovers' Lake. You looked very involved."

"Talking to Oscar . . . Oh, yeah." Ian almost managed a smile. "Same old Oscar. It was almost like old times. He used to depend on me to help him in his courses when we were in middle school. I don't know how he got along the last few years. I don't suppose he tried very hard. But it was just like the old Oscar. He needed to find something out and he always took the easy way, you know, asking around until somebody knew the answer instead of really doing some research."

"Oh." I was disappointed. "Was it just for a class assignment?"

Ian nodded. "Yeah. But he was really taking it seriously, trying to get it right. I told him he should call and talk to my Dad because I wasn't really sure. I think he did."

"Your Dad?"

"Yeah."

"What does your Dad do, Ian?"

"He's the District Attorney, Ms. Farrell."

I gripped his arm. "Ian, what did Oscar want to know?"

Ian looked surprised. "Oh, it was pretty technical stuff, Ms. Farrell. He wanted to know how you can prove criminal conspiracy." Ian frowned in thought. "He said, what if a couple of guys robbed a bank, broke in at night and busted the safe and got away with a million bucks, but they didn't leave any physical evidence behind, no finger-prints or bloodstains or anything like that, and nobody saw them. He wanted to know if one guy could turn the other in. I said sure, he could, but one party to a crime couldn't be the sole proof against another party to the crime."

I must have looked blank.

"You have to have some corroborating evidence," Ian explained. "Something more than just the co-conspirator's word. Something. Like some physical trace at the crime scene or. . . ."

"A witness," I said excitedly, "a witness. How about a witness who hears the conspirators discussing the crime?"

"Sure," Ian said quickly. "Yeah. That's what Oscar wanted to know. He latched onto that idea, too."

Witness. That was the key to Oscar's plan. He was going to have a witness. Me. A witness to two conspirators discussing their crime, then, presto, there would be independent knowledge of their guilt. But the witness hadn't come. And Oscar's co-conspirator had had plans of his own. Very detailed and violent plans.

The stakes must have been very large. Oscar had indeed known something his killer would do anything to prevent becoming known. It hadn't been some sexual peccadillo. No, it was more dangerous.

The Rabbit was hot. I unrolled the windows and waited patiently for the long string of cars to inch their way out of the cemetery. I had plenty of time to think on the way back to Friars' Academy.

What in the world had Oscar been involved in?

A bank robbery?

Surely not. Surely that was just an example Oscar had used with Ian. He wouldn't have told him a bank robbery if that had actually been the case, would he? But, to tell the truth, I could see Oscar participating in a bank robbery. It would be exciting, different. And to get away with it!

Had there been any recent bank robberies in LA that had occurred at night with no physical evidence left behind? Bank jobs were usually afternoon heists. Alonzo could find out very quickly.

Perhaps the bank robbery had been an example. What other kind of crime could it have been?

Robbery, murder, theft, smuggling, extortion, arson, the possibilities were myriad and surely Alonzo was better equipped than I to seek out criminal activity on the campus.

That's what I told myself, but I couldn't keep from worrying it in my mind. Classes resumed at eleven o'clock. I talked, asked questions and answered them, but the hour was a blur in my mind. I kept thinking of the kind of billboard with moving parts where the picture changes as the slate revolves, different colours blending to make another image. Face after face expanded, broke and reformed in my mind. A coconspirator. A man. A man I knew.

Who, among these cultured civilized people, was a criminal? Of whatever kind.

Clay Fredericks. My mind came back to him. I could not see Clay robbing a bank or engineering a theft or arranging an extortion. If Clay committed a crime, it would have to be easy and low key, nothing sordid or unpleasant or actively dangerous.

Pat Porter. Pat was certainly high-strung, a volatile personality. Would anybody in his right mind conspire with Pat?

Paul Casteel was another story. We knew Paul was a bookie. Was he something more? Could he and Oscar have committed a crime together?

Alonzo came in as my eleven o'clock class began to disperse for lunch.

"Are you free for lunch?"

I was.

"I thought we might pick up some hamburgers and go to the Brevard Gardens. A picnic."

We did a little better than that. We stopped at a nearby delicatessen and bought Greek sandwiches, two bottles of Tuborg and a bunch of fresh seedless green grapes.

The Brevard Gardens, endowed a half century ago by the shipping family, covered a five-acre stand in the heart of La Villita. Palms and flowering shrubs and artfully cultivated wildflowers combined in a subtropical paradise. We parked in one of the perimeter lots and walked a half mile along a shaded path to a shallow lagoon that shimmered in the midday sunlight. I carried the lunch and Alonzo a plaid picnic blanket.

As he spread it out over a cushion of pine needles, I asked dryly, "Do you always travel with a handy blanket?"

He looked up at me, his dark eyes intent. "Only when I intend to have a picnic with a beautiful girl."

I sat with my back against a stump and shared out the lunch. "Is that supposed to disarm me?"

"It's a start," he said through a mouthful of ham, provolone and pita bread.

I laughed and he did, too.

I told him what I had learned from Ian that morning, but then we left murder behind. We talked quickly, there was so much to say. It was altogether too short an hour. In fact, it was an afterthought, as I was getting out of his car at the Administration Building, that he said, "I'll see you around three. I've asked Dr. Howard to call a special faculty meeting."

"Why?"

"It's time to stir up the animals. I'm not having any luck yet in finding out what Oscar was involved in. It won't do any harm to open it up, let everyone know what we're looking for. It may make someone nervous."

I met with my one o'clock class then ran a batch of copy downtown to the job-printer who published the *Herald*. I was a few minutes late for the faculty meeting. The heavy oak doors to the conference room, next door to Dr. Howard's office, were already closed. I opened them quietly, ready to slip unobtrusively to my seat if Alonzo was already speaking, but the click of the opening doors swung every head toward me. There was an infinitesimal easing of tension when they saw me. It was extremely quiet. Alonzo wasn't here yet and they were all waiting uneasily for him. Dr. Howard's chair was still empty, too.

As I slipped into an empty seat, Paul Casteel said loudly, "Well, if it isn't the law's best friend."

"For heaven's sake, Paul," Dodie Wingate said sharply, "you always teeter on the edge but this time you've gone over it."

Paul cocked his head and looked at Dodie. "Have I? You mean you like having a spy on the faculty, ready to relay everything she knows to the cops?"

Belinda Bascomb's pop eyes widened. "Why would Ann have anything to do with the police?"

"Let's ask her," Paul suggested silkily. "Ann," and he nodded formally at me, "why don't you tell us why you are such chums with the police?"

The silence around the table was intense, absolute.

Belinda stared at me and so did Clay and even Dodie.

"If we're going to answer questions, Paul," I retorted, "why don't you tell us how you earn your pin-money?"

His face hardened.

134

"Come on, Paul," I jibed, "tell us about your nice set-up here. Tell us how you skim money off the students."

One side of his mouth quirked up in a humourless smile. "The little fuckers can afford it."

"Sure they can. But how long will the Board of Trustees keep you on, Paul, after they find out?"

"They wouldn't find out if it weren't for you and your boy-friend," he said angrily.

"Ann's boy-friend?" Belinda repeated.

"Our own Lieutenant Fox, Belinda love. The very same fuzz who's going to put one of us in jail for killing Oscar. With a little help from Ann."

Belinda's head swung toward me. "Have you told . . . ?" Her face began to flush a mottled ugly red. She pushed back her chair. "Ann, if you've . . . ."

The double doors opened. Dr. Howard walked in, followed by Alonzo.

Once again it was absolutely quiet.

Dr. Howard looked from Belinda to me and back again. "Miss Bascomb, what is wrong with you?"

"Nothing, nothing," Belinda mumbled and she subsided heavily into her chair, but her eyes, those pop-eyed blue eyes, clung to my face.

Dr. Howard took his place behind the lectern and began to speak and, abruptly, he had everyone's attention.

". . . find myself in a difficult position. I am not in sympathy with the purpose of this meeting." His voice oozed distaste. "I have made it clear to Lieutenant Fox and I want to make it clear to all of you that I do not believe a Friars' Academy faculty member has been or is involved in a criminal conspiracy of any nature."

It was intensely quiet. Every face was turned toward Dr. Howard.

"However, it is incumbent upon me to cooperate with the authorities. I have made it clear to Lieutenant Fox, nevertheless, that I may find it necessary to talk to our school attorney, Mr. Leonard Fitch, if I decide Lieutenant Fox's inquiry is exceeding proper bounds."

With that, Dr. Howard sat down.

Alonzo stood and looked down the long polished table. He looked tough, capable and determined.

"One of you," he said finally, almost casually, "is a murderer. You know it and I know it. I'm going to find you."

He paused. Someone rustled uneasily in his chair and the sound was strikingly loud.

Alonzo looked at each of us in turn. "One of you committed a crime at some time in the past and Oscar Charles Howell II knew about it, was a part of it. For some reason, Oscar decided he was going to see you in jail. He made a plan."

They hung onto every word.

"We know that Oscar intended to trap you. He had arranged to meet you in the *Herald* office Thursday afternoon. He did meet you. But then his plan went wrong. He had expected Miss Farrell to be there, to overhear him discuss that crime with you."

Heads swivelled toward me, then back to Alonzo.

"But Miss Farrell didn't receive Oscar's message asking her to come. So he was alone."

Alonzo frowned. "I would have thought Oscar would be wary of you, but, somehow, you persuaded him to step out onto the balcony. I suppose he was so big he wasn't afraid." Alonzo's eyes ranged around the room. "Now, I want to say something to the rest of you. I want you to listen carefully." He paused. The tension was as palpable as the atmospheric pressure before a storm. "Murderers are like rattlesnakes.

136

They'll strike if you step near them. No matter who you are or whether you intend them harm or not. So, if any one of you knows anything, anything at all, come and see me. It may not be anything big. Maybe it's just a little piece of knowledge. Like a teacher owning something too expensive for his income. Or maybe you saw somebody at an odd place at an odd time. Some little thing. Whatever it is, don't keep it to yourself. Don't be a victim."

FOURTEEN

There was a general swarm toward the door. I was going against the current, intent on reaching Alonzo. No one spoke to me as I passed and I was quite aware of sidelong hostile glances. I lifted my chin and kept right on going. There was, after all, something slightly haywire if it was better to protect a murderer than to consort with the police. To hell with it.

I fell into step with him. "Alonzo, what about Jason Horvath?"

Alonzo looked blank.

"Oscar's best friend. You talked to him Friday. He's the weedy kid with the mirrored sun-glasses."

"Oh, yeah. High voice. Acne. Nervous."

I nodded.

"He said he hadn't seen much of Oscar lately. He didn't have any idea on who might have killed him."

We came out of the Administration Building and blinked in the afternoon sunlight. Alonzo touched my elbow and we started down the steps.

"Then why did he come to see you?"

Alonzo shrugged. "It was more that he was curious to know what was going on. Wanted to know who I suspected and whether I had any idea what Oscar might have been doing at the *Herald* office."

"What did you tell him?"

"Not much."

We walked for a moment in silence then I asked, "Who do you suspect now?"

"Everybody. Nobody. I have men checking the financial background of some of your people. Maybe somebody's not reporting some income. That would give us a lead."

That reminded me of the Fredericks.

"How about Clay and June? Have you found out where their money comes from?"

"They aren't the gentry," Alonzo answered. "As a matter of fact, Clay must hustle a little harder than he seems to. Their money's from vending machines."

"Vending machines?"

"You know," Alonzo explained, "coin-operated laundromats and candy and cigarette machines. It's very profitable."

So the money belonged to Clay and it wasn't from a southern fortune. I tried to imagine Clay scooting around La Villita in his Jaguar, cleaning out the backs of coin-operated machines. It didn't picture easily. Probably he hired somebody to do the picking up.

In the *Herald* building, Alonzo and I parted at the foot of the winding stairs. I turned down the curving hall into the news-room. It was empty this afternoon. I supposed none of the kids were in the mood to work after the funeral this morning. I wandered around, neating up, and listening as the front door opened and shut, opened and shut. Alonzo was getting some reponse from his plea for help.

Perhaps at this very moment, someone was walking up those curving stairs with the piece of information that would unravel the tangled thread of the investigation.

What had Oscar done that fell within the definition of criminal conspiracy?

I leaned against the horseshoe.

And whatever Oscar had done, how did it hook up with a

member of the faculty?

If I were going to imagine Oscar involved in a crime, I would look first among the other students for a partner. Didn't that make more sense? What faculty member in his right mind would depend upon a pothead like Oscar?

Jason Horvath. I could picture him so clearly. His jacket never quite fitted. It hung from his bony shoulders, sagged across his narrow hips. His tie was a regulation medium-width brown knit but it was always lumpily knotted and looked lopsided. Jason and his mirrored sun-glasses. They were armament as protective as a hooded visor. You couldn't really see Jason. The sun-glasses hid his eyes, hid his thoughts and fears and visions.

On impulse, I swung around and lifted up the telephone receiver and rang a familiar number.

She answered on the first ring. "Mrs. Wingate."

"Dodie. This is Ann. I want you to check Jason Horvath's file for me."

"Ann?" Her voice was cool, distant.

"Dodie, what's wrong?"

"I didn't know you were in that cop's pocket."

"Now, look, Dodie . . ."

"What have you told him about me?"

"Nothing that will harm you," I said quickly. "Besides, Dodie, you can relax. He's looking for a man. Not a woman."

"Oh," she said slowly. "Oh, thank God. Ann, I'm sorry. I didn't mean to turn on you, but I've been so dreadfully afraid."

"I know. But you can relax. He's getting close to the end of it."

"Really? Are you sure?"

"Yes." Then I said teasingly. "Of course, if I weren't in the cop's pocket, I wouldn't know these things. Maybe you'd rather not hear. I wouldn't want to compromise your principles or anything."

"Drop dead," and she sounded like the Dodie of old. "All right, Ann, you want to know all about Jason Horvath. How come?"

"I think he should know something. Of course, he told Alonzo . . ."

"Who?"

"Lieutenant Fox."

"Ah ha. Alonzo now."

"Rest your salacious mind. Jason told Alonzo that he didn't know from nothing but I find that hard to believe. I thought I'd go have a talk with Jason, but I've never had him in class and I don't know anything about him. What do you have hidden in the Academy's all-seeing, all-knowing filing system?"

"Hmm. Just a minute." The receiver thumped on her desk. I heard the high squeal of a metal drawer being pulled out and the rustle of paper. The drawer thudded shut. "Yeah. Here we go. He's been at the Academy since seventh grade . . . average grades but good test scores . . . considered an underachiever. . . no discipline problems but not well-liked by teachers . . . never actually does or says anything disruptive but his general attitude is unattractive." Dodie paused. "I don't know that I can get any closer to it than that. Helen Fischer, the French teacher, says he gives her the creeps. That's how he strikes everybody. The general feeling is that he's into drugs pretty heavily, but, once again, he shows up, does his work, at least minimally, and he doesn't lip off. So there's no complaint against him. He's even been on a partial scholarship the last few years. His Dad died, a car wreck, and the school policy is to offer a scholarship to any past student with an acceptable record if the family becomes financially unable to pay."

"No insurance money?"

"Apparently not. His parents had a little real estate agency. Not one of the social ones that gets the big listings. It was a pretty modest operation and you know how high the tariff is here. His mother has gone to work for another group. She didn't try to keep their agency going, so her income is based on commissions. I guess she isn't making enough to keep Jason here."

"Where would Jason be now?" It was already almost half past four.

Papers rustled again. "I doubt if you can catch him today, Ann. He's in intramural volley-ball and that's dismissed at four. Do you want his schedule for tomorrow?"

"Okay." I wrote down his classes and thanked Dodie for her help. I could wait until tomorrow . . .

"Oh hell, Ann, you're incorrigible," I said aloud to myself and I snatched up the student directory. I found the address and was on my way.

Jason lived on a scruffy street in a small frame house. The sleek low-slung black Trans-Am in the drive looked distinctly out of place.

I pulled in behind the sports car. Jason was squatting in front of the car, polishing the grill. He heard the Rabbit and looked up and slowly stood. He turned his face toward me and the sunlight glittered on the mirrored lens. He made no move to come toward me.

I got out and walked up to him.

"Hello, Jason."

"Hello, Ms. Farrell."

"That's a pretty car. Is it yours?"

"Yeah."

I reached out, lightly touched the shiny black paint. "It

must be fun to drive a car with so much power."

Those glittery opaque lens never moved. He made no answer, just stood there next to the car, his thin face solemn, one hand tightly clutching a wax-softened cloth.

"Where did you get the money to buy this car, Jason?"

He shifted his weight from one foot to the other. "Just like anybody, Ms. Farrell. Working. I got a job. I make payments."

I was shaking my head. "Not that car, Jason. It cost too much for you to qualify for a loan. I wouldn't be surprised to find out it's all paid for. And, what's funny, Jason, is that you don't drive it to school. I've never seen this car at school. You ride a mo-ped, don't you? Because it might cause some questions to be asked if you drove this car to school and someone knew you attended on a scholarship. Isn't that right, Jason?"

"It's nobody's damn business," he said quickly. "Just because I go on a damn scholarship doesn't mean I can't have anything! It's my business."

I looked past him, at the small shabby house with its worn paint and sagging shutters and untended yard. "Is your mother home, Jason?"

"No. Listen." He took a step toward me, his face flushing. "You leave her alone."

"Where do you work, Jason?"

He hesitated, then shrugged. "I work for Mr. Fredericks, see. It's a good job, pays good. He's got this vending-machine business and I service the machines, put in fresh products and pick up the money."

I wished I could see through those mirrored glasses. It would be easy enough for Jason to rip off Clay. "How much does Mr. Fredericks pay you?"

Jason's mouth tightened. "None of your damn business, Ms. Farrell."

Had Jason stolen from his employer? Surely he couldn't have earned enough honestly to buy that Trans-Am. But even if Jason had skimmed money off the top of the receipts, how could that be involved with Oscar and whatever nefarious scheme he had pursued?

"Did Oscar work for Mr. Fredericks, too?"

Jason finally changed expression. He laughed. It wasn't an especially nice laugh. "Shit, no. Oscar was rich! Why would he want to go around milking a bunch of damn machines?"

There was certainly no good answer to that. I couldn't imagine either why Oscar would have wanted to do that.

I decided to go at it another way.

"Jason, you and Oscar were partners. We know that. If you want to protect yourself, you'd better tell the police all about it."

He shook loose a cigarette and took his time lighting it and all the while those damn silvery lens hid his eyes, made his face unreadable. He took a deep drag. God, I was impressed. I waited patiently. He blew smoke in a soft hazy curl, then said softly, "Bug off, Ms. Farrell."

It was very quiet. I could heard distantly the faint roar of the traffic on main street, and, farther away, the high cry of an afternoon freight.

I wasn't frightened. I couldn't be frightened of a skinny boy with acne and a weak chin, but I knew suddenly, I was absolutely certain, that I had touched on something evil.

We stood there for a moment longer then I turned away and walked back to the Rabbit and got in. After I had started the motor, I tried one more time.

"Jason, if you know what Oscar was involved in, you should know it was dangerous."

He just stood there.

"Jason, if you won't tell me, I'm going to talk to the police lieutenant. You will have to answer to him . . . and he may be very curious about how you afforded such a fine car."

"Gee, Ms. Farrell, you really scare me."

I jammed the Rabbit in reverse and bolted out of the drive. When I shifted into low and jerked forward, I looked in the rear-view mirror. Jason was still standing by the Trans-Am. As I picked up speed, I saw his head move, the sun glistening on those mirrored lens as he watched me leave.

Yeah, I was really scary all right. Jason was all atremble. But I wasn't finished with Jason.

I had to fight the five o'clock traffic so it was a quarter to six by the time I got home. I stopped just inside the door to check my box and pulled out a bunch of message slips and skimmed them. Mother. Sheila. Dodie. And Alonzo. Twice.

I called Alonzo first.

He was excited. "Hey, Ann, we're finally getting somewhere and it looks like Pat Porter. Which surprises the hell out of me."

It did me, too. Pat had been acting like a scalded cat but murder!

"What's Pat done?"

Alonzo gave a short laugh. "I can see why he's been nervous about his fiancée. If she ever finds out . . ."

"Finds out what?"

"Pat's been acting in some porno movies. Acting in and making them. Saves paying a skin actor. Improves profits."

"Well, it's not the kind of thing you list in a bio but do you really think Connie Contreras would care all that much? The way she holds onto him, I would think. . . ."

"But they are fag flicks."

"Oh. Oh and oh."

"This is all just a tip right now but I'm working with Jim Vincente in Vice and he's getting a search-warrant. The headquarters, studio and cutting-lab, are supposedly upstairs behind this gay disco. We're going to raid it at seven tonight."

"How would Oscar tie into all that?" I asked slowly.

"We'll find out. Once a case starts to break, you'd be surprised how quickly it all comes out."

"Maybe. But Alonzo, I'm pretty sure Jason knows what Oscar was into. In fact, I think Jason was in on it too. Let me tell you how he acted when I went by his house this afternoon."

Alonzo listened, but, I had to admit, my report was pretty small beer in comparison to the info on Pat Porter.

"Yeah, well, I'll check into it. But, like I said, Ann, once we find out a little we usually find out a lot. By this time tomorrow, we may know the whole story."

The whole story.

I tried to fit the pieces together. Oscar helping to make gay flicks? Oscar, I was sure, wasn't gay. Or, if he was, he liked all kinds of sex because I knew what kind of message I'd always received from him. If I had indicated the slightest willingness to play, we could have had something going. But I didn't have Jennifer's fancies. Of course, I wasn't Jennifer's age, either. So I wasn't making a judgment. I was just looking at it the way it was. The way I was. Now. There had been so many unexpected twists in the lives of the people I knew, Dodie bedding with Clay, Jennifer's youthful chums, Paul Casteel's bookie-service, Bitsy's sad secret, that I certainly didn't feel able to make any hard assumptions. And certainly not about Oscar.

Oscar and a criminal conspiracy. He had talked to Ian about bank robbers. Could he have meant porno purveyors? But that kind of crime certainly resulted in physical evidence. All he had to do was get his hands on the films. And was it the kind of crime Oscar would have tried to use against someone?

Not someone. Pat Porter. Why would Oscar, if he and Pat had worked together in that lavender world, have decided to turn on Pat and try to destroy him?

There could only be one answer to that, no matter how I perceived Oscar's sexuality.

I hadn't believed Oscar would write poison-pen letters. Did I believe he would help make fag flicks? Well, I could see the movies before the letters.

Could Oscar's depression and anger have been because of a lost love, but not the loss of Bitsy?

I reached over and turned on the Tiffany lamp that sat on top of the oak bookcase. The varicoloured glass panes glistened cheerfully but it didn't do much to lessen the early evening dusk and, when I looked in the dressing-table mirror to brush my hair, my reflection was as dim as the room. And as imprecise as my recollection of Oscar. Who was Oscar and what was he? Was he a devoted loving grieving friend of Bitsy's? A maladjusted neurotic teenager with a boiled head venting his bile in poison-pen letters? A sexual deviate driven by who knew what passions? A conspirer in crime hounded by remorse?

The telephone rang.

"Hello."

"Ann, I'm glad I caught you," Dodie said. "We're just going out but it occurred to me, and I don't know that it makes a difference but it's another link between Jason and Oscar, that you might not know that Jason and Oscar crewed the last two summers on the *Miranda*."

"The *Miranda*?"

"The *Miranda* is Clay and June's yacht. And believe me, Ann, it's really a yacht. Teakwood in the cabins and velvet curtains in the saloon." She paused. "That's boatese for living-room."

"Thanks, Dodie. I wouldn't have known. Having, of course, grown up around here, I hardly know a thing about boats."

"All right, all right. Listen, I have to run. Seth's honking. But I thought you might want to know."

"Sure." I had known vaguely that the Fredericks had a yacht and that Oscar had travelled with them. It had come up casually one day. But I hadn't known Jason was along, too.

The gong sounded in the lower hall signalling dinner. It wasn't required that I eat with the boarders regularly but it was only good manners to make it to the dinner-table two or three times a week because part of my job was to serve as a link between the faculty and the live-in students.

I swiped the brush through my hair, put on a fresh coating of coral lipstick and flew down the stairs. Dinner was always fairly leisurely because the students alternated as waiters and that didn't make for speedy service.

The entrée was corned beef and hash. I wondered idly what I had missed eating the last couple of evenings for that would be the basis of this particular dish. I took a very small helping and filled up my plate with green salad. While we waited for our waiter, a junior from Duluth, Minn., to clear the plates, I turned to Bobby Harris, a senior from Tacoma.

"Bobby, do you know Jason Horvath?"

Bobby has a bland cherubic face with pink cheeks and a huge shapeless mouth usually stretched in a good-natured grin. He hesitated for just an instant, then said, "Sure, Ms. Farrell, I know everybody in the senior class."

"Do you know him well?"

"No." Bobby looked abruptly less cherubic and faintly alarmed.

"Can you tell me someone who does know him well?"

Bobby moved uneasily, then looked over his shoulder.

"Hey, excuse me, Ms. Farrell, but it's my night to bring in dessert. I'd better get on out to the kitchen."

Bobby did bring desserts in a minute, depositing sticky dishes of rice pudding at each place, but he didn't put one down for himself and he didn't come back to the table.

I pushed the lopsided mound of pudding back and forth in my dish, talked about Jane Fonda's new movie, then turned down coffee and excused myself. I looked for Bobby in the student lounge and in the library. I stood for a moment in the downstairs hall as students milled by, some on their way to Fine Arts for a Charlie Chaplin movie, some to the gym for a basketball game, but I didn't see Bobby Harris.

A cool uninflected voice called my name, "Ms. Farrell."

I looked around. Sonja Gerson was looking at me out of limpid grey eyes. Sonja always reminded me of a tortoiseshell cat I had when I was little. She was slightly plump and wore her long blond hair straight and loose. She looked wise, aloof, and, always, faintly amused.

"It's cooler out on the verandah," she observed.

I followed obediently behind her. She led the way to a couple of wicker chairs at the far end. As we sat down, Sonja shook her blond hair, letting it settle around her shoulders, then, once again, she studied me out of those huge grey eyes.

"It was very interesting to watch Bobby's reactions to your questions. At first, he was merely wary, then uneasy, then panicked. Quite interesting." She sounded like a lecture circuit psychiatrist on the Good-Morning-America show.

"You found it interesting?"

"Yes." She tilted her head and looked at me unblinkingly. "Didn't you?"

I shrugged. "Not especially."

"But you want to know about Jason. Doesn't it make you wonder when an All-America type like Bobby gets nervous just talking about him?"

"Do you know why?"

"Of course."

"Why?"

"Drugs." She watched the sudden interest in my face with amused satisfaction.

"Jason takes drugs?"

She looked impatient. "Of course, Ms. Farrell. But that's not the point. Who doesn't?"

I could have mentioned a few.

"Nobody cares who *takes* drugs. But nobody wants to admit they know who *sells* them."

Drugs. Conspiracy. Oscar and Jason. A yacht. Facts shifted and settled in my mind. How simple it was if we only looked at it right side up.

A conspiracy, of course, but one that made all kinds of sense. Oscar would like the thrill of smuggling. That would entertain him. Not the prospect of money but the excitement of circumventing the law. And Jason, well, Jason could use money and the Trans-Am proved that he had.

It was a beautiful theory, perfect as a circle. All I lacked was proof. I left Sonja, and raced up to my suite.

I looked up the number. I had never called it before.

"Hello." Her voice was as precise and unruffled as her tennis.

"Hi, June. This is Ann Farrell. Is Clay there?"

"No, he's at the club. He plays in a men's doubles league on Monday nights."

Monday night. We had buried Oscar only this morning. It seemed a hundred years ago. Of course, there was no reason why Clay should forgo his game just because it was the day of Oscar's funeral.

"Can I help you?" June asked pleasantly.

Well, of course she could. But did I want to tell June of my suspicions? I hated to upset her, but she would learn of it eventually if I were right. I hesitated then decided to plunge ahead.

"June, you go along with Clay on his summer cruises, don't you. On the *Miranda*?"

"Yes."

"You and Clay took Oscar Howell and Jason Horvath with you last summer and the summer before, didn't you?"

"That's right. They received the trip in exchange for working as the crew."

"Where did you go last summer?"

For the first time, she paused. "What's this all about, Ann? Why do you want to know?"

"June, I've had . . . well, it's a brainwave! I think I know what's behind Oscar's murder! I was talking to another student and I found out that Jason sells drugs. We knew that Oscar was involved in some kind of criminal conspiracy with the person who killed him. . . ."

"What do you mean? What are you talking about, Ann?"

There was nothing for it but to tell her the whole story from my discovery of Oscar's note asking me to meet him at the *Herald* office to my talk with Jason Horvath.

"Don't you see? It all adds up. Everything fits. Jason and Oscar must have smuggled a load of pot back here last summer. At least, that's my theory—and it all hinges on where the *Miranda* went."

"Oh. I see." She paused for a long moment. "I suppose it could have happened," she said unwillingly. "We went to a half dozen ports in Mexico and Colombia, but, Ann, I would hate to think the boys would have done something like that. In fact, I just can't believe it!"

"I know," I sympathized, "and, if it turns out to be true, it

151

was certainly ungrateful of them to take advantage of you and Clay in that way. But the *Miranda* is a big boat, isn't she? There would be plenty of room for them to smuggle something aboard, wouldn't there?"

"Oh yes, yes, it could be done," June said reluctantly. "Clay and I used the master cabin but there are three other cabins forward and two aft. Yes, there would be plenty of room. Oh, Ann, I certainly hope this isn't true. Clay will be awfully upset."

I appreciated her concern but I doubted that Clay, easy, pleasant Clay, would be terribly troubled. It would be too bad, of course. It might prompt him to hire a professional crew in the future, but, as long as it didn't touch him, I doubted that Clay would be overcome with emotion. However, I said all the right things.

"What are we going to do?" she asked finally.

I looked over at my electric clock. A quarter to seven. Alonzo would already be *en route* to raid that backroom studio.

"I'll call Lieutenant Fox. The first thing in the morning."

FIFTEEN

But I didn't talk to Alonzo the first thing Tuesday morning. It was still dark when the phone rang. I thrashed awake and grabbed up the receiver and, at first, couldn't make any sense of the unfamiliar voice speaking so quickly and with such an undertone of fear.

". . . never stayed out all night before. Never. He is so good to tell me when he will be home. And he said he would only be gone a little while. Where is he, Miss Farrell?"

I flicked on my bedside lamp and pulled a pillow up behind me. "What are you talking about?" I asked foggily. "Who is this?"

"This is Alma Horvath. I told you. Alma Horvath. I want to know where Jason is."

That woke me up. "How should I know?"

"But he went to meet you. Last night. And he never did come home."

That was all she knew. The phone had rung, just after eight o'clock. Jason had answered. She didn't hear all of the conversation, just a bit.

"He said, 'Tonight?' in kind of a surprised voice, then, 'Sure,' and 'Okay.' He came back into the living-room, we were playing Scrabble, and he said he had to go out for a little while. I asked if it was his job, sometimes he has to make night deliveries, but he said no, it was a teacher at school, Ms. Farrell, and she wanted to talk to him about Oscar, something about Oscar's murder. I asked him how long he would be gone and he said just a little while. But he never did come home."

Jason had walked out and climbed into his black Trans-Am and driven off into a cool January night and never returned.

"Have you called the police?"

"No," her voice answered, "I thought I would call you first. Oh, Miss Farrell, where is he? What time did he leave you last night?"

"I didn't see him last night, Mrs. Horvath. I didn't call him."

"But Jason said. . . ."

"I don't care what Jason said. I never called him. I talked to him yesterday afternoon. About four. But not later."

"Who called then? And why did Jason say it was you?"

I had no answer for either question. Had Jason thought I called him? Or had he said the caller was me for reasons of his own? I didn't know. Only Jason knew.

Where was Jason now?

I called Alonzo at home.

"Ann!" he said immediately. "We really hit the jackpot in that studio. The Vice squad is going wild. We haven't hooked Oscar into . . ."

"Alonzo, something's happened to Jason Horvath!"

He was blank for a moment, trying to switch from Pat Porter and the porno-film raid to Jason. I told him about Jason's mother's call and then what I had learned from Sonja and June last night and my conclusions.

"Drug dealing!" Alonzo exclaimed. He was quiet for a moment, then he said slowly, "It could be. It just could be. And now Jason's disappeared." He drew his breath in sharply. "For God's sake, Ann, and you went out there and faced him all alone."

"Oh, I'm not afraid of. . . ."

"Ann, don't you see it? If he's the partner, Oscar turned on him. He's the killer."

"Jason?"

"Hell, yes. That's what it looks like to me. Especially if he's taken a flyer."

"Do you think he told his mother I called just to confuse things and that he has deliberately run away?"

"Why not? It must have been pretty clear to him that he was close to being caught."

"But if he really went to meet someone . . ."

"He had to have some excuse to leave. But we'll find him."

I went to school early then waited impatiently to call Dodie's office and ask her if Jason showed up.

He didn't.

It was a long dreary morning. It started to rain about eleven. Alonzo dashed in after lunch.

"We're going all out to find Jason. I've put out an arrest call on the teletype. The LAPD are looking too. It's already hit the radio and TV stations so we've started getting calls. We'll pick up his trail soon." He looked tired. "Let's go through it again, Ann. Tell me what happened at Jason's, every word."

I tried to recreate for Alonzo the moment in time that I spent on Jason's driveway. When I was done, he was puzzled. "There wasn't much to it, was there? But the fact that he's gone means you really scared him."

"I didn't think he was scared," I said dubiously.

"If we knew what was in his mind. . . ."

"No," I said decidedly, "he wasn't scared. Wary and tense, but not scared."

We left it at that. Alonzo promised to pick me up at six for a drink and dinner. After he was gone, it seemed lonelier and drearier than ever in the deserted *Herald* office.

It was marvellously cheering when the kids trickled in for my one o'clock class, but it was over too soon and I was alone again.

When the front door sighed open, I looked up eagerly.

Clay came around the curve, water dripping from his umbrella. He shook it, closed it and hooked it to a chalk-board tray. "Ann, what's all this about Oscar and Jason? June told me when I got home last night and I don't mind telling you frankly that it's knocked me for a loop. Your cop friend came with a search warrant to look over the *Miranda*. Of course, I told him he didn't need a warrant. Nobody wants to clear this up any faster than June and I. And we just can't believe the boys would do something like that! What did Jason say?"

Of course, it came down to the fact that Jason had said very little.

Clay pounced on that. "It looks to me, Ann, like this is all supposition on your part. Just because Jason has a car and Sonja likes to be dramatic."

Sonja did like to be dramatic, but the Trans-Am was a fact.

"I don't see how Jason could buy that car on what you pay him to service coin-machines!" I objected.

"I don't suppose he could. But his mother may have had some money to loan to him. You've jumped to a lot of conclusions, Ann."

"But Jason is missing. People don't run away for no reason."

Clay shrugged. "Who knows what some crazy kid will do?"

I was staring out of the rain-smeared windows. "Or get killed for no reason," I added sombrely.

That brought Clay's head up. "You don't think someone's

killed Jason? That's absurd."

"Is it?"

"Of course. He'll show up. He's just off on a kick. Hell, teenagers today . . ."

"His mother said he'd never stayed out all night before."

"There's always a first time."

But we weren't really talking about an evening on the town and we both knew it.

Clay pulled out his pipe, slowly filled it. When he had it lit, he took a deep puff. "I don't care what you say, Ann, I don't believe Oscar and Jason were involved in selling drugs."

"Why not? It's not especially out of character for either of them."

"That's true enough," Clay admitted. "Though June and I would like to think, since we spent so much time with them, made such an effort, that something of our care touched them. But kids have a knack for separating their actions from their consciences. When they have consciences."

"But you and June didn't have any idea . . . ?"

"For God's sake, Ann," Clay said reproachfully.

"Oh, I know you wouldn't have tolerated that kind of thing. I meant, looking back on it now, do you remember anything suspicious?"

Clay looked at me thoughtfully. "There was one funny thing . . ."

They had docked about five one sultry June evening at Buenaventura. The boys had taken off early in the evening to explore the town and they had been late getting back.

"We were getting worried," Clay said.

The next morning, before they sailed, two Indians had delivered a straw chest to the *Miranda*. Clay had been about to send them away when Oscar came up from below and said it was for him. It had taken Oscar and the two men to carry it aboard.

"At the time I just thought it was one of those odd purchases a kid can make, a big ungainly ugly wicker chest. God knew Oscar didn't have any use for it but I didn't really think about it because there was plenty of room aboard and Oscar could afford whatever he wanted to buy. But, now, looking back on it. . . ."

It's always easy, looking back, to understand a lot of things.

"Hell of a thing," Clay said wearily. "Those nice kids . . . and then to have one turn on the other. . . ."

"But that doesn't explain the telephone call."

Clay looked blank.

"The woman who called Jason last night."

"Oh, that could be anybody. A girl-friend. A wrong number. Nothing at all. It gave him an excuse to get out of the house."

"Do you think they will find him?" I asked abruptly.

Clay looked surprised at the stress in my voice. "Hey, Ann, don't take it so personally."

I turned and walked across the room to stand and look out into the soggy streaming afternoon. "How can I not? Whatever happens is my fault! If I hadn't gone over there yesterday afternoon. . . ."

Clay came up behind me, slipped an arm around my shoulders. "Hey, little girl, don't be upset. And you're wrong, you know. None of this is your fault. You're an innocent bystander."

"A culpable meddler, I'm afraid," I said unhappily.

"Nonsense. Look at it this way, Ann. If Jason's gotten himself into a bind, it certainly isn't your fault." He hugged me. "Now, come on, Ann, be happy. Here we are, together on a rainy afternoon. I can't think," and his voice was soft, "of anywhere I'd rather be than here with you." He tilted my face toward him. "You are so lovely, Ann. Does every man tell you that?"

I looked up at his smooth handsome face, the wiry blond hair so thick and touchable, the vivid compelling blue eyes.

"And what do you tell every girl, Mr. Baker?"

The hand touching my chin was suddenly rigid. He drew his breath in sharply and there were, abruptly, two white thin lines bracketing his mouth.

I jabbed a little harder. "That apartment must lack a little for assignations. Is the furniture maple?"

"Ann, how the hell . . . ?"

We still stood so close together but there was no intimacy now. It was the first time I had ever been near Clay and not sensed sexual undertones.

"Someone who knew Bitsy saw her going in there one Sunday afternoon. And she knew Bitsy was meeting an older man."

"Who?" The harshness of his voice surprised me.

"That scarcely matters now, does it? Besides, the girl didn't know you were the man. I suppose I'm the only one who knows."

"What do you intend to do about it?"

"For heaven's sake, Clay. Nothing, of course. What good would that do? I don't even know why I brought it up now." But, of course, I did know why. It had made me angry, his automatic try, and I had determined to break that sleek sensuous composure. Now I was sorry. His face was so white, so stricken.

He swung away from me. "Dammit, Ann, I didn't know she was pregnant. Dammit, I didn't know. I got a letter . . . but it was too late then." He turned, faced me, and his eyes filmed with tears. "Why didn't she tell me?"

"I'm sorry, Clay," and I was.

159

"I would have. . . ." But his voice trailed off.

I looked at him curiously. He wasn't so handsome now, but, paradoxically, he was more attractive because there was real grief in his face.

"What would you have done?"

He jammed his hands in his trench-coat pockets, shook his head uncertainly. "I don't know exactly . . . we could have run away . . ."

Run away. Oh my God, was that the best he could imagine?

"You could have gotten a divorce."

He looked at me then his eyes, such brilliant deeply blue eyes, slid away from mine. "June . . . I don't think June would let me have a divorce."

It isn't all that difficult to divorce here in the land of milk and honey and incompatability.

Had Bitsy sensed this with a knowledge beyond her years? When she was up against the reality of a pregnancy had she known in her heart that Clay would never leave June?

"Do you love June so much?"

"I don't know," he mumbled. "It's hard . . . you don't understand . . . everything gets so complicated." Yes, I knew that. Money is complicated and people are more so. His life was tangled with June's and perhaps he hadn't seen any way to break apart.

"But it's too late now," he said dully. "It doesn't make any difference now."

The rain splashed against the windows and it was a lonely sound like a river of tears. It was still raining at six when Alonzo came to pick me up. We considered staying in my suite, I could fix omelettes, but we decided to go on out. We went to Mama Kate's, a seafood restaurant on a pier in Santa Monica. It was a long drive but worth it and, sitting out over

160

the choppy water with rain and sea-spray slapping against the windows, we ate succulent fried shrimp and drank Tuborg and my edge of depression began to lift.

I didn't tell Alonzo about my interlude with Clay. I wasn't especially proud of it and I hated remembering the empty look on Clay's face when he left the *Herald* office.

Alonzo was tired. "Nothing. Absolutely nothing. You'd think the kid had gone up in a puff of smoke." Then he grimaced. "Of course, there are a million places to hide in LA. Or he may be drinking Dos XX's in Tiajuana right now."

"You think Jason killed Oscar?"

"Maybe. At the very least, I'd say he was afraid of getting busted. I've had Petree and a couple of other men talking to Academy kids all day. Dodie Wingate suggested kids she thought were likely customers. I'd say your info is right on point. Everybody gets very quiet, damned quiet, when we start asking about dope and Jason and Oscar."

"So Oscar and Jason were sellers?"

"It looks that way. And it looks like Jason must be the one Oscar was trying to set up for a rap. Though it still seems funny. Even if Jason were shorting him. It meant Oscar was gambling on going state's evidence or was even willing to go to jail to get Jason canned. If that's the case, then Jason is the killer."

"If you catch him, will you charge him with Oscar's murder?"

Alonzo took a last bit of cole slaw. "That's where we're in trouble, Ann. We don't have any physical evidence yet. We searched Jason's house today but there wasn't anything to link him to the *Herald* office and Oscar's murder. The DA's going to have to have more than we've found so far. But we're still looking and, who knows, maybe we'll get a confession."

I remembered Jason standing in the drive, the sun glinting

on his silver-lensed glasses. Somehow I doubted that Jason would be too cooperative when he was picked up. If he was picked up.

The rain was easing into a smoky mist as we drove back to the Academy. I invited Alonzo up for a nightcap. We took a moment in the foyer to shake the water from our raincoats and wipe our feet. I glanced towards the pigeon-holes to our right and a queer electric tingle of shock raced through me.

Yes, it was my slot and the brightly pink slip of paper tucked in it was unmistakable. I snatched it out and unfolded the single sheet. Alonzo read over my shoulder.

> Dear Ms. Farrell, I need to talk to you. I don't know what to do. It's about Oscar. Please meet me at the *Herald* office tonight at ten. If you call the cops, I won't be there. Come on foot so I'll know you're alone. Thanks. Jason H.

"It looks like his handwriting," Alonzo said. "I looked through his school books today and I'd almost swear he wrote this."

"Oh, Alonzo, that means he's all right. I've been afraid. . . ."

But he wasn't listening to me. He was staring down at the note, his face grim. "I don't like this. I don't like it at all." He glanced at his watch. "It's almost nine. That gives me an hour."

"What are you going to do?"

"I'm going to close up this campus so tight, a mosquito couldn't get out."

"Wait, Alonzo. He'll know if you bring a lot of police and cars . . ."

"Ann, I know how to do these things. He'll never know anyone's around." He looked back at the note. "The *Herald*

162

office. That's pretty well thought out on his part."

Jason had chosen his spot well. He could be waiting in the line of cedars, well hidden, and he could see both the main parking-lot and the paths leading to the *Herald* office.

Alonzo spent an intense fifteen minutes on the phone and everything was set up. At a quarter to ten, he nodded at me. "I'll go with you until the path comes out in the open."

We didn't talk as we walked down the soggy path from McDonough Hall to the foot-bridge. It was utterly deserted. I turned on my flashlight as the path dipped toward the edge of the barranca and the bridge. The broad boards of the hanging-bridge glistened wetly in the gleam of the flashlight. I moved a little ahead of Alonzo, leading the way.

The bridge gave an odd little sideways lurch as if it had sagged a couple of inches.

I felt as if a fist had exploded in my chest. Because I knew. I had crossed this bridge a hundred times, more than a hundred times. I began to scream when the bridge yawed sharply to the right.

"What the hell," Alonzo shouted.

And the bridge ahead of us, with one last sharp lurch, tore away and we began to fall.

SIXTEEN

There was an instant of sheer horror. As the bridge collapsed, plunging us down into nothingness, I heard the rattle of the boards, like giant dominoes clicking down, and a thin high scream and Alonzo's shout. I threw away the flashlight and tried to grab the thick manila rope that served as a handrail. Even as I flailed to my right, I knew I was too late. Oh God, how stupid! If I had carried the flashlight in my left hand, held onto the handrope with my right . . . But it was too late and I was going to fall and fall and fall . . . Alonzo was twisting violently and I thought, he's kicking me, why is he kicking me? Then, with a hard hurtful jerk, his legs locked around me. I couldn't breathe but I wasn't falling any longer. I was dangling, helpless and terrified. I knew how far below me the boulders waited. We swung slowly, in a lazy sickening arc.

"Ann!" His voice boomed, echoing off the walls of the barranca, "Ann, hold on!"

But I couldn't. His legs pinioned my arms against my sides and, even as we swung, so lazily as if it didn't matter, I felt myself begin to slip, my slick raincoat sliding against the polyester of his slacks.

Alonzo felt it, too. "Grab my foot, Ann, grab it!"

If I slipped away from him, if I fell, I would plummet forty feet into the sharp-edged scree along the barranca floor. Desperately, I struggled to reach up. My nails tore against his slacks. I tried so hard in a final frantic try, I clutched his ankle

164

but I knew I couldn't hold on.

I was going to fall, there was no way, no hope . . .

Alonzo pulled up his leg, dragging me along, then a strong hand gripped my wrist, locked onto me. "Come on, Ann. Up. That's the way. Up." I reached out, clutched the dangling remains of the bridge, found a toe-hold on the slatted crosswalk and both of us hung like limpets and tried to breathe again.

"Jesus," he said softly into my hair.

I pressed against him and tried to stop trembling.

"It's all right now," he said quietly. "We won't fall now, Ann. All we have to do is hang on. We're all right now."

I still pressed as close to him as I could. I knew in my mind that we were safe but my body was still afraid.

It was only a few minutes, though it seemed interminable as the bridge swayed and eddied, before Alonzo's shouts brought a startled nightwatchman, his flashlight bobbing, to the lip of the barranca. It was a longer half-hour before we were finally hauled to the top by the La Villita fire department.

Alonzo paused long enough to be sure I was all right then he and Sergeant Petree began to climb down into the barranca. I huddled in a blanket offered by a paramedic and drank hot coffee and watched the play of spotlights up and down the steep green slope and waited.

Alonzo found the wire-cutters resting on top of a tangle of shrubbery midway down. He showed them to me before a laboratory technician took them away. They were ordinary wire-cutters but shiny new. "It was so easy," he said grimly. "Two wires were sliced through, just like cheese. Two others were weakened. When we walked far enough out, bam."

It was almost midnight when the fire-wagon and the three squad cars and the ambulance pulled out and the barranca lay darkly quiet and Alonzo walked me slowly back to McDonough Hall.

I fixed us both a drink. I sank down onto the sofa but Alonzo paced up and down the room, taking an absent-minded swallow now and then.

"Not a trace," he said explosively.

And there hadn't been. Jason, if it was Jason, had come and gone as invisibly as a wraith.

Alonzo stopped in front of the couch. "You won't be safe until we've caught him."

I was so tired, so depleted by shock, that I didn't answer, but my mind still gave a wriggle or protest. Jason?

"A real killer," Alonzo was saying grimly. "He didn't even worry about someone else crossing the bridge before you."

"That depends upon when he clipped the wires."

"What difference would it make?"

"If he didn't cut the wires until after nine, he could be pretty sure I would be the one who fell."

"Why?"

"The kids in McDonough Hall have to be in the building by nine."

"Oh. Oh, I see. Dammit, we must have just missed catching him. I sent for the squad cars to set up surveillance at nine, but they weren't in place until at least nine fifteen. He must have made it off the campus just before they came."

That's the way it stood. There was no trace of Jason on the campus but Alonzo searched my suite before he left, checking and locking all the windows. "Ann, for God's sake, don't take any chances. No funny phone calls or odd-ball trips, do you understand? This kid must be a psycho and now he's really desperate. I want you to promise me that you won't hare off to meet him somewhere."

"You don't," I said wearily, "have to worry about that."

166

It was still raining the next morning. The rain slapped softly against the huge long window-panes of the *Herald* office.

Alonzo dropped by just before my eleven o'clock class. "We haven't come up with any leads on Jason yet, but you don't need to worry, Ann. He's not on the campus."

He stood close to me and I wanted so badly to reach up and touch his face, but the students were beginning to come down the hall, pulling off their raincoats, grousing about the weather.

"You'll stay on the campus for lunch." It wasn't quite a command.

"Yes."

"All right. I'll be around to get you at four. Okay?"

I caught a glimpse of Alonzo as I walked back to the *Herald* office after lunch. He was walking briskly toward the Administration Building, head ducked against the rain. I wondered what he was doing now. I felt secure, knowing he was on the campus. It made it easier to spend the afternoon alone in the *Herald* office.

The phone rang about two.

"Ann!" There was a frantic edge to her voice. I knew immediately that something was wrong.

"June, what is it?"

"Ann, my God, I'm so frightened." Her voice was thin and high. "I don't know what to do."

"June, take it easy. What in the world has happened?"

"Please, Ann, you've got to help me. You can tell me what to do. You know that policeman . . . I have to talk to you."

"Of course, June," I said soothingly, "of course, I'll talk to you. But what's happened?"

Her voice dropped to a whisper. "Something happened last night."

"June, what are you talking about?"

My voice was so sharp she didn't answer. I said more quietly, coaxingly, "June, tell me, what happened?"

"Wait, wait a minute." Her voice faded as if she turned from the receiver. Then it came back. "Oh God, it's all right. I was afraid he had come back. I've got to get out of this house."

"What happened last night?" I asked insistently.

"He was so angry." Now she began to whisper again. "He came home from school and he told me that you were a meddler, a menace. Then he went out, oh, it must have been eight-thirty or so and he didn't come home until almost ten. He told me I was to swear that he had never left the house last night. The way he looked . . . Ann, I'm afraid!"

You're afraid, I thought, with a cold emptiness. I'm the one here on the campus, alone in the *Herald* office and it was just this time yesterday afternoon that he came. Oh my God, you're afraid!

I came back from a frightful distance to hear her final words, ". . . meet me and help me decide what to do."

"Meet you?"

"Yes, I told you. I need to talk to you. And there's something I want to show you. Then you can help me decide what to do."

It was just after two. Alonzo wasn't coming by until four. There would be plenty of time to meet June then come back . . . I didn't want to come back to the campus. Not alone. Not even with June. Not if Clay were here.

Where was Clay? Was he in his office right now? Or was he even now walking across the campus through the rain, hidden beneath a black umbrella, anonymous and unnoticed in a trench coat.

I could meet June and then we could make plans, perhaps

go directly to the police station.

"Meet me in the Safeway parking lot. On Santa Fé. In fifteen minutes."

I tried to call Alonzo before I left, but he wasn't at the station or on the campus. I wouldn't come back to the campus until I'd gotten in touch with him. Not so long as Clay Fredericks might be here.

When I stepped out of the *Herald* office, I looked around very carefully, but the paths were deserted, the rain hissing steadily down.

I ran, splashing through puddles, drenching my sandals, and I didn't feel safe until I had reached my VW and locked the doors.

I drove slowly across the wooden bridge. As I passed Callison Hall, my eyes fastened on the bright square of light that marked Clay's offices.

I took a deep breath when I curved onto the main boulevard. God, I was glad to be getting out of here! I slowed at the main gate. There was a police cruiser parked there. I was almost through the entrance when I saw its driver look up sharply and gesture at me.

Had Alonzo left word I wasn't to leave the campus? I waved at the cruiser. I'd explain when I called him.

I drove slowly, the winding road slick and treacherous from the rain, but I drove automatically, my mind absorbed with Clay. Handsome, charming, smiling Clay.

So I'd been right, after all. It made the best kind of sense now. Of course, Jason and Oscar hadn't run a drug ring by themselves. They had been directed and controlled by an intelligent, calculating adult.

Clay. He loved rich, fine clothes, luxurious appointments, magnificent cars. He had vending-machines, sure, and weren't they handy to explain his swelling wealth. And Oscar had been involved all along. I could see that. I liked Oscar but I could see him as a smuggler. Oscar would think it was a blast, a real blast. And, of course, he liked Columbian pot for himself, too. I doubted if Oscar peddled it. That wouldn't have been his style. Oscar would've liked the excitement of conspiracy. It was Jason who wanted money from selling dope. It bought him a Trans-Am.

It must all have rocked along, smooth and easy, until Clay made a huge and, ultimately, fatal mistake.

Clay seduced Bitsy, the girl Oscar loved and admired and revered. Bitsy must have told Oscar in that final pathetic letter and Oscar determined on revenge.

Oscar wouldn't blacken Bitsy's memory or break her parents' hearts. No, he wouldn't do that, but he was determined to make Clay pay. And he knew how to do it. Clay loved money but money isn't too helpful in prison. There aren't any cashmere sweaters or mirrored bedrooms in prison.

Oscar set about it very carefully. He knew Clay was guilty of smuggling. All he had to do was get his proof. I was going to be the witness. Did he intend for me to be hidden and overhear as Oscar talked to Clay about the last shipment and how much it had earned?

Yes, Oscar had it planned. He made only one mistake. He hadn't realized how far Clay would go to protect himself. Clay must have realized his peril. Had Oscar already threatened him, just after Bitsy's death? So Clay planned ahead, wrote the anonymous letters, and, when Oscar made the appointment for that final afternoon, Clay had come to the *Herald* office with a short sharp knife and a clean packet of the pink warning notes.

I stopped for a red light at the foot of the hill. Yes, Clay was very, very clever. And he might have gotten away with all of it if Jason hadn't bought a Trans-Am. I turned right on Santa Fé.

Jason. Oh God, where was Jason now? I was terribly afraid I knew. Clay couldn't take a chance that Jason would talk. I was very much afraid that Jason was dead.

And me? I had come very near death. What a horrid shock it must have been to Clay yesterday when I called him Mr. Baker. Not only because it meant that I knew about Bitsy. Worse than that, I knew about the apartment that he kept as the centre of his drug dealing for I was sure now that was the reason for the apartment.

No wonder Clay had tried to kill me.

The red neon of the Safeway glimmered through the rain. I slowed and turned into the asphalted parking-lot. I peered through the rain and saw someone standing beneath an umbrella on the far side of the lot. I eased up beside the car and it was June. She reached out and opened the door and climbed in, closing her umbrella.

Usually she was such a fashion plate. I was surprised at the shapeless fit of her dark brown raincoat and dark scarf. She must have grabbed the first thing she found from her closet. But her gloves were a delicate pink and expensively cut.

"I was afraid I'd miss you," she said breathlessly. "I had to borrow my maid's car." She nodded toward a seedy Ford. "Mine wouldn't start." She began to pleat the edge of her scarf and looked at me imploringly. "Oh Ann, do you think it can be true?"

I was sorry for her. I didn't know her well and certainly had no emotional attachment to her, but it would be ghastly to have your world crumble around you as June's was doing. Her face showed the strain. Her mouth was taut with fine lines at the corners. She was pale beneath her make-up and dark purplish shadows splotched beneath her eyes.

I couldn't meet her gaze directly.

"June, I'm afraid so. I'm afraid so," and I told her how it looked to me.

She didn't say a word while I talked but, at the end, she nodded heavily. "Have you told the policeman yet?"

I shook my head.

She sighed. "We will have to, won't we?"

"Yes."

She fumbled in her pocket. "Ann, look at this. This is what I wanted to show you," and she slapped a tagged key onto the car seat.

I knew what it was, of course. Hotel and motel keys are unmistakable. I read the inscription, SnuggleTimeInn, 397 W. Fresno. I looked up at June.

"This was in his raincoat pocket," she said tensely. "Last night. When he came home."

What was I to say? If she hadn't figured Clay out by this time, she was a fool. And, obviously, she had known about Bitsy so perhaps she knew about all the others.

"I want to go there," she said grimly.

"To the motel?"

"Yes. I know it has something to do with all of this."

I didn't think so. We would find an empty motel room, the bed neatly made, the bathroom with paper-covered glasses, an empty closet.

"Look, June, we need to call Al . . . Lieutenant Fox. This can wait."

"No. No, it can't! I'm going to the motel first. I have to know," and her voice was rising.

She was close to breaking apart. I knew that, could feel it in the tension here in the car, see it in the wild light in her eyes.

I looked down at the motel key. 397 W. Fresno. It was only a few blocks from the police station. We could go there and, once she saw the empty characterless room, I could call Alonzo or perhaps we would just drive directly on to the police station and have his office find him.

I turned the windshield wipers on to sweep away the film of rain and drove out onto Santa Fé. It was one block to Fresno, which doubled as State Highway 101. The SnuggleTimeInn was three blocks west halfway up a hill. I fell in behind an oil-tanker that growled into low gear at the foot and strained toward the crest. I turned into the motel lot. The motel was L-shaped and Rm. 53 was on the backside. I eased into the parking-lot. There was one other car, half the length of the building away. Several doors down, the cleaning-cart rested half-in and half-out of a doorway.

"It doesn't look like there's anybody here."

But June's face was set and determined. She was already getting out. I got out too and came up behind her as she knocked on the door.

I started to speak then waited as a truck laboured up the hill. It would be hard to get a good night's sleep at the SnuggleTimeInn. But I doubted Clay had been in search of sleep.

June jammed the key in the lock and turned it. I could see a dim room. She pushed the door open and stepped inside and switched on the light. It was just as I had expected, a motel room like thousands of others, dark green cover on the double bed, formica-topped bedside table, a brass coloured lamp, a TV set, a dresser with a Gideon Bible.

I stepped past June. "There's nothing here," I said gently. I walked toward the bedside table and the telephone. I was reaching for the receiver when I saw the bathroom door start to open.

He looked just as he had yesterday, his cheap brown slacks wrinkled, his too-big sports shirt loose and misshapen, his sunglasses glittery and shiny.

"Jason!"

"You should have minded your own business, Ms. Farrell," he said sorrowfully.

Behind me, I heard the door slam and the rattle as the chain lock slid home.

I jerked around.

June looked so big and strong and formidable, standing in front of the door, and the blue-black gun that she pointed at me was as steady as her voice. "Yes, Ann, you certainly should have minded your own business."

Death stood there, watching me.

"You can't get away with this!" but my voice was thin and high.

June almost smiled.

"Someone will hear . . ." The rest of my words were drowned out as a truck rumbled up the hill outside and, with a sharp explosive blast, backfired twice.

"Oh, I've thought it all out," June said easily.

And she had. I had almost glimpsed the truth but it was June, not Clay, who planned it. It was June with the tough, determined personality. Clay liked rich but he liked easy, too.

Did Clay even know? I doubted it. I could see now how it had happened. Oscar threatened Clay. It was Clay he wanted to destroy, but, in his overpowering single-minded anger, Oscar had forgotten about June, June the co-conspirator, the co-smuggler, the co-enjoyer of all the money and all the luxury. If Clay went to prison, June would go, too. She could be sure that Clay wouldn't try to protect her. She knew him well enough for that. Exposure by Oscar would signal the end of ease and comfort for June, too.

"You planned it all. You wrote the anonymous notes."

She nodded. "I thought it out very carefully . . . and it was working until you ruined it."

She was going to enjoy pressing that trigger and watching me fall. She was looking forward to it. I could see it in her face.

"Oscar asked you to meet him that day . . ." I began hurriedly. Stop that finger, hold it, keep it from moving.

"Oh no. Oscar asked Clay to meet him but Clay told me. Clay always tells me everything. He didn't know what to do. He was so upset." There was a world of disdain in her voice. "I told him I would take care of it. I did. I planned very carefully."

What would have happened if I had been there according to Oscar's plan? I swallowed sickly. Death had been so close to me these last days and now I faced it across the room. There was nowhere to go, no place to hide. I couldn't look away from the small dark hole at the end of the gun barrel.

"What did Clay do when he found out you'd killed Oscar?" If I could keep her talking until . . . But time wasn't going to help either. Except it was all the time I was going to have.

"Clay doesn't know. I told him I went to the office and found it empty. Oscar must have already been killed. Clay believed me, of course. He always believes what he wants to believe."

Easy Clay.

"All right now." Her voice was suddenly crisp, purposeful. Like an efficient chairperson. "Over here, Ann."

I looked at her warily. Come and be killed. I'd be damned if I'd make it easy for her.

But I had made it easy, hadn't I? Running to meet her, bringing her here. Oh Lord, why hadn't that cruise car stopped me?

"Sit down, Ann. In that chair," and she waggled the gun at

the green slip-covered easy chair.

"No."

Her eyes flared. She raised the gun.

I looked toward Jason. He still stood in the door way to the bathroom, but his hands clutched the frame and he was breathing shallowly.

"Are you just going to watch, Jason?"

"Ms. Farrell," and his voice was hoarse and thick. "What can I do?"

"Come here, Jason."

He looked at June warily. She was nodding toward the writing-desk.

"Get out some motel-paper, Jason. You're going to help me."

Slowly he walked to the desk and got out the paper then looked at her.

June frowned in thought. "Okay, Jason, write this down."

He picked up a pen.

"Write, 'Dear Ms. Farrell . . .' "

Jason looked puzzled. "What for, Mrs. Fredericks?"

"You remember," she said patiently. "I explained it to you. When they find her body, they have to have some reason why she came to the motel. And you'll be long gone, Jason, on your way to Rio. You don't need to worry about it."

I looked from him to her.

Jason bent back to the desk and June again started to dictate. "Dear Ms. Farrell, I can't go on. I'm . . ."

"Jason, no!" I screamed. His hand jerked against the paper. "Jason, don't write it, don't!"

His head snapped up.

June drew her breath in sharply and raised the gun until it was level with my heart.

"Don't you see, Jason?" I demanded. "Don't you understand! She's going to kill you! That's your suicide note."

He swung around and faced June and saw the truth in her face.

"Mrs. Fredericks, no!" he cried. "No, please, no. I'll do whatever you want, I'll do anything!" She began to walk toward him and he backed away, his hands outstretched in front of him.

I looked down at the bedside table. Could I reach the ashtray? It was solid and heavy, clear white glass. If I threw it hard enough, fast enough . . .

Jason was against the wall now but she had stopped and the gun moved back and forth between us. It was dreadful the way I could read her thoughts. My time was up now, all over and done with. She was going to shoot me first, then, while the shock of it held, she would lunge forward and press the pistol against his head and Jason would die, too.

One, two and we would be done, no threat to her and the murders so neatly solved, Jason so carefully implicated. Who would be surprised at his suicide?

Her hand went up. The deadly hole of the gun barrel pointed at me. I watched and it seemed to grow bigger and bigger. I flung up my hands.

The sound of the shot rocked the little room.

177

SEVENTEEN

Alonzo wrapped his arms around me. "You little damn fool, you little damn fool," and he said it over and over again.

"I didn't know," I mumbled defensively, but I was clinging to him with all my might. I didn't look as they led June from the room, her hand swathed in a thick bandage, her shabby raincoat splattered with blood, her eyes wild with hate.

We went to the police station. They took my statement and I knew someone else must be talking to Jason. It took a long time and I was very tired, but I was conscious every moment of Alonzo's nearness and it buoyed me up.

Finally, they were through. As we left, I made him tell me again how he'd been there to save me.

"Well, of course I had your line bugged. It seemed a cinch Jason would call."

But it wasn't Jason.

"And other things were breaking. I never thought two kids could run a dope ring on their own. It figured the Fredericks were in on it. We had men tracing their money and that began to look good. Then the lab found a blond hair entwined on those wire-cutters. Jason was never a blond. Further, it was dark at the roots. That let out lover boy. Then you got that call and off you went."

We were halfway up the hill toward the Academy by now. He was shaking his head. "You went haring off! I told you to be careful, didn't I, Ann?"

"I didn't think of June," I said in a small voice.

"If ever there was a case," he said sternly, "of the female being deadlier than the male . . ."

But I wasn't interested in that. I wanted to hear again how he had been there just in time.

Alonzo grinned. It was the first time he had smiled that long afternoon and his face was vivid in the pale night-gloom.

"Like the Mounties, huh. Okay," and he told me again patiently. "The cruiser followed you until I could pick up your car in my unmarked Ford. I kept circling around that damn supermarket until you started off. That was the dangerous part. If we'd lost you . . ."

But they hadn't. Once at the motel, Alonzo had taken the manager's pass-key, gone in Unit 52 and eased open the connecting door.

"So, really, I had it under control. Hell, Ann, I wasn't going to let her shoot you!"

So he said he wasn't a hero.

But I knew better.